HAUNTED HOUSES

CHILLING TALES FROM AMERICAN HOMES

THIRD EDITION

by Nancy Roberts

Old Saybrook, Connecticut

Photo Credits: p. 11: Ruth Keyes; p. 43: courtesy of Old Fort Niagara; p. 53: courtesy of Governor's office, Dover, Delaware; p. 67: courtesy of Ashton Villa Historical Association; pp. 85, 93, 104, 114, and 157: photos by Bruce Roberts; p. 99: courtesy of Germantown Historical Association; p. 129: photo by Mary Waddington Smith; p. 137: photo by Susan A. Bush; p. 143: courtesy of Cedarhurst Club; p. 149: photo by Evelyn Prouty; p. 171: courtesy of Inn By the Sea; p. 178: courtesy of John Stone's Inn. All others by the author.

Library of Congress Cataloging-in-Publication Data
Roberts, Nancy, 1924–
   Haunted houses : chilling tales from twenty-four American homes / by Nancy Roberts — 3rd ed.
     p. cm.
  ISBN 0-7627-0320-2
  1. Ghosts—United States. 2. Haunted houses—United States.
I. Title.
BF1472.U6R634   1998
133.1'0973—dc21
                                           98-24362
                                             CIP

Manufactured in the United States of America
Third Edition/First Printing

CONTENTS

PREFACE

There are houses that you and I should, perhaps, never enter—houses that can be lived in with only the greatest understanding and tolerance.

Within them we may encounter ghostly presences, soft touches from invisible fingers, eerie sounds, the echoing footsteps of unseen inhabitants, pervasive fragrances, or even vile stenches.

There are those of us who are skeptical, but there are others who would not mind saying that, perhaps, these houses are haunted. Where are they, and what is it like to live in one of them? How do the owners adjust to curiosity seekers, to the skepticism of their friends, and, most of all, to sharing their home with an apparition?

The pages of this book contain stories written in a style that will be not only easy to read but especially suited to being read aloud. They are accounts of hauntings, presences, and spectral appearances obtained from interviews conducted across the country. If you were to ask me what sort of people I talked with, I would have to describe them as ordinary people. They were down-to-earth, intelligent, and, probably, very much like yourself. In this book, I have let them tell their own unique stories.

There is often an impression perpetuated—intentionally, I believe, by so called "ghost hunters"—that spirits return because of violent circumstances or for revenge. I would say this is not necessarily true and is entirely too limiting and unimaginative. As a writer who has probably researched more ghost stories based on personal interviews than any other author, I have become convinced through conversations with those who claim supernatural encounters that there are as many reasons for the appearance of a ghost as there are kinds of people—or should I say spirits?

Nor do I believe that these ghosts are necessarily tragic spirits trapped somewhere in space, unable to enter either heaven or hell. Rather, I believe that they are sometimes the recipients of an occasional and very special dispensation.

I have just returned from the most recent in a series of excursions that have taken me all over the United States in search of special houses with memorable ghost stories. Tonight, I sit writing by the light of a small brass-and-emerald-glass student lamp that belonged to my great-aunt. It is a reminder of the many times I lay beside her in bed at night as a child and coaxed, "Aunt Jess, tell me a story." From her prodigious memory she would hold forth, and I was enthralled.

Not all of the narratives herein are suitable for bedtime, but that will be up to you to judge. Here is how one of the stories I wrote for this collection begins:

When the moon is full above the Castle on a summer night— that is when they say it happens. And for all we know it may be happening tonight. Pray it won't. Or pray, at least, that neither you nor I will be there to see it if it should.

There is much early history of our country in this story, and that is one of the reasons I enjoyed writing it.

Most of the stories in this book are about places you may tour, in which you may spend the night, or which you may at least drive past and wonder about. (Please respect the owner's privacy when doing so.)

And now, dear reader, here is your opportunity to visit some unforgettable houses!

THE HATCHET MURDERS

The Lizzie Borden House,
Fall River, Massachusetts

Sheets of rain wrapped the car obscuring Phil's view of Interstate 95, and drops fell with a staccato rap on the roof of the new Chrysler van as they made their way from Wareham to Providence. Marcie wiped mist from the inside of the window beside her. "It is really bad, Phil. Why don't we stop and spend the night somewhere?"

"It isn't that far to your sister's now. We can be there in another two hours, if the rain lets up."

"And if it doesn't? Phil, the radio just said this storm is the edge of a hurricane. The Fall River exit should be coming up soon, let's turn off there."

"And stay where? I don't know anything about Fall River."

"For some reason the name sounds familiar," said Marcie. We could try a B&B. That would be a pleasant part of our trip."

"Marcie Rollins, only you would think of making a funeral trip *pleasant*."

"Well, we don't need *two* funerals. Ours, from having an accident in this downpour, and my brother-in-law's, too."

"That's true. Does Cindy need you tonight?"

"I don't really think so. Bob's sisters are there at the house." Another barrage of rain pummeled the van, and the headlights of other cars became more difficult to see between the rivulets of water on the windows. "I'm going to give her a call on the car phone and tell her about this weather, Phil. Isn't the Fall River exit coming up?"

"Yes. I'm going to take it."

The answer at the first B&B was not encouraging. "We don't even have that small room left, do we Amy?" the owner asked his teenage daughter. She shook her head. "People leaving the interstate to get out of the storm, I guess."

"Do you have any suggestions?" asked Phil.

"There's the one at 92 Second Street," suggested the girl. "Of course they're nearly always full up, but you could try them." She suddenly giggled and said, "If you don't mind staying there." Her father gave her a reproving look.

His directions were clear, and a few minutes later they were peering through the rain at the front of an austere two-story frame home. Narrow as it had looked when they drove up, it went back farther from the street than they had realized and was actually quite spacious.

"You're lucky tonight," said George Quigley at the desk. We usually have reservations a long time ahead, especially during the month of August, but these people," he tapped a name on his register, "I'm sorry to say they've had a death in the family and had to cancel. We can give you their room. It's the guest room, the one where Abby Borden's body was found."

"Bad weather out there tonight, isn't it," he commented, shaking his head. "How about some cold cider for you, or milk and our homemade cookies? We have pears, too, of course."

"Milk and cookies sounds great," said Marcie, placing her suitcase beside the stairs. "Wasn't the way he said *pears* strange," she said to her husband after their host had left for the kitchen.

"I didn't think about it one way or the other."

The Lizzie Borden Bed and Breakfast Museum where controversy still continues as to Lizzie's guilt or innocence.

The milk and cookies appeared almost instantly and the Rollinses sat down on a black horsehair sofa.

"The furnishings of this house are just remarkable!" exclaimed Marcie, reaching for a cookie.

"Oh, do you like them? We researched to find authentic pieces from the 1850s," said Martha McGinn, one of the owners. "Some of the furnishings were either originally in the Borden house or are very similar in style."

"Oooh, look at this cookie. What a strange shape," exclaimed Marcie.

"Don't be rude, honey. It must be for Washington's birthday," said her husband.

"In August?" exclaimed Marcie.

"Hatchet-shaped cookies are one of our specialties. And, of

course, August is special, too. Since today is the fourth, we have had our anniversary reenactment of the hatchet murders of Andrew and Abby Borden. I'm sure you've read about the famous crime."

"A crime here," Marcie said breathlessly.

"Now, we understand if that makes you nervous, Mrs. Rollins," said Kathi Goncalo who works at the desk, "and we have a list of other bed-and-breakfast places." Phil could hear the moan of the wind and rain beating against the windows, and he had visions of driving through it to discover that accommodations were nonexistent. Of course they could drive back to the highway to one of the chain motels. "We really are not nervous," he said with a smile.

"Well, sometimes people are. Especially with the history of the house you know."

"I'm not," said Marcie. "I think it's absolutely fascinating. I love mysteries."

"I thought that might be why you and Mr. Rollins came here."

"Actually, we're refugees from the storm," said Marcie.

"So it wasn't because you wanted to spend the night at the Lizzie Borden Bed and Breakfast after all."

"Lizzie Borden? That name sounds familiar," said Phil.

"Oh, yes," said Marcie. "I remember it all. Poor Lizzie was suspected of murdering her father and stepmother. Now I know why the name Fall River had such a familiar ring when I saw the sign on the interstate." And that's the reason for the hatchet-shaped cookies!"

"I don't see why it should upset us now," said Phil. "It all happened over a hundred years ago, didn't it?"

"Yes, one hundred and five years ago this month. I'm glad you and your husband aren't scared, Mrs. Rollins. I think what bothers people the most is not that there was a double murder here but that it occurred in such a gruesome way."

"As if people consider some murders not as bad as others?" said

Marcie thoughtfully. "That's an interesting idea, isn't it Phil?"

"Not to me, Marcie. I feel horror over any murder . . . it breaks one of the laws of God. I'm not sure I'll ever understand your interest in crimes."

"It's just that I'm fascinated by any type of mystery. You know that."

"Especially one that has never really been solved," said a guest who was sitting in a nearby easy chair listening. "Hope you don't mind my interrupting, but everyone has a different theory, Mr. . . . Rollins; Is that right? My name is Bernard Breckenridge."

"How do you do," said Phil. Breckenridge continued. "And they say that after it happened, some couples actually divorced over disagreements about who did it. Imagine that!"

"How ridiculous." said Marcie.

"Let me show you some of the interesting things in the house, Mrs. Rollins," said George, offering them cider, cookies, and fruit. "Why don't you take this pear up to the bedroom with you, Mr. Rollins. You may decide you need a snack later." Phil Rollins hesitated. "Do take it. We always keep plenty of pears on hand. It was Lizzie's favorite fruit and she said she was eating pears out in the yard under a tree at the time the Bordens were murdered."

"But I thought she was supposed to have . . ." began Marcie. "Killed them?" said longtime employee, Kathi Goncalo. "No one really knows and probably never will. Lizzie was certainly a prime suspect, but she had a good lawyer and was acquitted."

"And what do you think, Mr. Breckenridge?" asked Marcie curiously.

"I'm not sure. Sometimes I think she did it alone, and sometimes I wonder if she didn't have an accomplice. A man whom she began to fear later. Everyone has a different opinion."

"We'll have a tour of the house in the morning," said George, "and point out where all the members of the family and the maid were supposed to have been when the crime took place. Why don't you stay and see what you and your husband think, Mrs. Rollins?"

"Wouldn't that be terrific, Phil?"

"We don't have time, Marcie. Maybe we can come back again."

"If it's not too late for you, Mrs. Rollins, let me take you through the house now and show you our modest library of books and crime scene photos."

"Do you mind, Phil?"

"Go ahead. I know you want to, Marcie. I'll go up to the room and read *USA Today.*"

"Fine, honey. See you soon."

"Are you sure this won't bother you before retiring, Mrs. Rollins?"

"Not a bit! Let's go."

Phil took their luggage up to the bedroom. It was really like walking into the world of his grandparents, he thought as he gazed at the old-fashioned furniture. Everything was just perfect. The bed and its pillows edged with crocheted lace, the bureau cloth, a white linen towel with a fringe. All very quaint. He was glad now that they had stopped here. He put the newspaper on the bureau and placed a small alarm clock from his overnight bag on the bedside table. A meticulous man and an experienced traveler, he never trusted the clock in the room or a wake-up call anywhere he stayed. Then he took out his pajamas and fresh clothing for the following day.

Suddenly he noticed that the room was cold. It had not seemed chilly when he came in. Well, no matter, he would just lay his new L.L. Bean robe across the chair to put on while he sat and read.

He began to unbutton his shirt and as he did so turned toward the old-fashioned oak bed. His fingers stopped at the second button. His hands began to tremble. The appearance of the bed was very different from only a few minutes ago when he had entered the room. Instead of the coverlet being perfectly smooth it was now quite rumpled. But that was not the important change. Its folds were rearranged so that they corresponded to the curves of a body, and it was not a slim body. On the pillow he saw an indentation that could only have been made by a human head!

Marcie returned to find her husband sitting fully dressed in the downstairs sitting room. His face was very pale.

"Why are you down here?" she asked in surprise. "I thought you'd be in bed by now, honey."

"Marcie, come upstairs. I want to show you something when you go in."

She stared at him in bewilderment as he put the key in the door of their room. "If something is wrong, why don't you tell the owners? I'm sure they will take care of it."

"Because I thought you should see this first. Look at that bed!" Dramatically, he flung the door wide and stood aside while she preceded him into the room.

"I'm looking. What's the matter?" she said a bit impatiently.

"The bed. The bed is what's the . . ." He stopped in midsentence. The pillow was plumped up and the coverlet was as smooth as it had been when he first entered the room . . . the room where Abby Borden was resting when she was brutally murdered more than one hundred years ago.

Next morning Phil sat in embarrassed silence while Marcie related his experience over a hearty breakfast of oatmeal, orange juice, eggs, sausage, and johnnycakes.

"Ooh, how wonderful. Why doesn't something like that ever happen to me?" moaned one guest.

"I've heard some people have woken up in the night to see a woman in Victorian clothes dusting the furniture, and some have even had her straighten the blankets over them as they lay there."

Martha McGinn noticed that Phil Rollins's face was quite white and he did not seem interested in his food. "Incidents are sometimes reported here by the staff but seldom guests," she said comfortingly. "People who work in the house say they hear the sound of footsteps or doors opening and closing mysteriously, but I think any spirits we have around here now are friendly ones. Visitors like to discuss their theories about the crime and they ask lots of questions."

"I have my own idea of what happened," said Marcie. "I scanned some of the books and bought a transcript of the inquest documents. You should read it, Phil. I think I know who murdered both of them and it wasn't Lizzie at all!"

The Lizzie Borden Bed and Breakfast Museum is thought to be a house "active" with spirits. Some guests have reported hearing voices and the sound of a woman weeping. Others tell stories of unexplained footsteps and doors mysteriously opening and closing. In addition to reservations for overnight accomodations, in summer the Borden House is open 11:00 A.M. to 3:00 P.M. daily for half-hour tours. It is located at 92 Second Street, Fall River, Massachussets 02721 (508–675–7333).

THE NORTH ROOM

Red Brook Inn, Old Mystic, Connecticut

There will always be houses that we pass on the road and say to ourselves, if I had a real home to go back to it would look like that and the presences of some of the people who once lived in that house would still be there. They would watch over me. The two brothers were about to stay in that sort of place.

Historic Haley Tavern circa 1740, and the Crary Homestead, built about thirty years later, are nestled on seven acres of wooded countryside on a hillside overlooking Route 184 and Welles Road. Albert Clodig and his brother, John, drove through the wooded New England countryside on a road just outside of Mystic. "That's the Crary house," said Albert. "I was drawn to it from the moment I saw its picture." A winding drive led up to the large center chimney farmhouse. It was a warm New England red, set back from the road on pastureland enclosed by stone walls.

"When was The Crary Homestead built?" asked John.

"In 1756, during the day of the adventurer Aaron Burr in this country. But with your love of music, you will probably say to yourself, 'Ah, I shall be sleeping in a house built the same year the great Austrian composer, Mozart, was born.'"

"I shall do just that when we are warmer," agreed Albert, "for I find this weather quite cold for March and am looking forward to a blazing fire within."

"And bread and pie baked in a brick oven" said John. "Did I mention that?"

"We are so glad to see you," said Ms. Keyes. She turned to Verne Sasek, her late husband, and asked "Would you take them up to the North Room, dear?"

"I'm eager to see Mystic and look forward to our two days here before my concert in Manhattan," said John. A professional organist, he was on his way to the city to give a recital at St. Thomas Church but Albert had prevailed upon him to visit Mystic instead of going directly to New York. "You tell me this place is unique," said John. "Well, I know I don't take enough time to enjoy my life," he admitted. "Often I simply go from one place to another, never experiencing what the places I'm in are really like."

This experience in itself, will be different, he thought as he entered the Crary house.

A large fireplace cast an amber glow over the room as they entered. Looking around him he thought of old paintings he had seen. There were stenciled floors and iron door latches. Period furniture and lighting devices and New England glass and pewter all captured the spirit of a bygone day. How the rooms of the past had corners filled with dark, somber shadows that both surrounded the people and added dimension to them.

"And when do you cook over the embers on the hearth?" John asked Ms. Keyes. "Usually during the holiday season," she replied. "You must come back to visit us."

"I shall," he said, staring into the flames. "But now we must retire; Albert and I have much to tour tomorrow. The Mystic Seaport Museum, an aquarium, and historic houses that belonged to some early sea captains." The Clodigs went to their room. There were toilet articles on a washstand and bureau common in the late 1800s and a large four-poster bed with a thick down mattress stood beside a narrow slate blue door.

The Crary Homestead–Mystic, CT.

Since the March night was unseasonably cold, the Clodigs had requested that a fire be lit in their bedroom. Watching the hypnotic flicker of the orange flames, they soon nodded over their reading and fell asleep. Albert says he does not believe in ghosts but he recalls that cold Thursday night well. Sometime just after midnight he suddenly woke to see a figure standing in the corner of the room.

"Looking straight in that direction, I saw a woman with white hair and a dark shawl wrapped around her standing in the corner staring at us. For some odd reason, I just thought she belonged there."

The way he described the apparition was to call it "a pleasantry." "I didn't really think of it as a ghost," he said. For a few minutes the woman stood there, her hands folded in front of her, calmly gazing toward the bed. Then she disappeared. When Albert Clodig looked over at his brother, he saw that he was still asleep, so he did not wake him, but it was more than an hour before he went back to sleep himself. Nor has Albert been the only guest to see this mysterious lady, whose clothing and demeanor give the impression of a lady from the past.

Ms. Keyes herself has felt the presence of this person in the North Room. She describes one occasion when she and her daughter were unpacking boxes upstairs and she had the distinct feeling that a third person was there in the room with them.

"My daughter looked up and said, 'Mother, I don't think we are alone in here.' I didn't think we were either, but I was reluctant to admit it. More than one guest who stayed in the North Room has come to breakfast and told us that we have a presence in there, but no one has ever been frightened. In fact, a gentleman said, 'You have a friendly spirit in that room I slept in,' and then he sat down before the crackling fire and, unperturbed, he devoured a hearty country breakfast!

"None of the supernatural events, however, quite surpass a memorable birthday party I held here. The sea captain whom I bought the house from was getting ready to remarry," says Ruth Keyes. "His wife had died after a three-month illness—throat cancer—and eight months later he married his wife's best friend, who was also widowed. She did not want to live in the Crary Homestead, so he sold it to me and he moved into his second wife's home."

Ms. Keyes made the historic Crary Homestead part of her B&B complex, redecorating a suite of rooms for reunions, wedding receptions, and other private functions. About five years after his second marriage, the former owner was about to celebrate his seventy-fifth birthday and, aware of his affection for his home of many years, his wife called Ruth Keyes. She said that it was her desire to celebrate the occasion with a birthday party for him at the Crary Homestead.

"We made an appointment for her to come over so that we might plan the party, and I left the Haley Tavern to go with her to the Crary Homestead," says Ruth. "She wanted to plan the arrangement of the buffet, the bar, and the room for the cake and gifts. But the moment we opened the front door there was a terrible odor . . . like dead meat. It permeated the whole house. 'It wasn't there this morning when I left,' I said in consternation. My own living quarters were in the house and there had been no odor earlier.

"I immediately asked my handyman to go check it. He came up to the tavern later that day and said, 'Ms. Keyes, there isn't any odor there!' About a week afterward the lady came back so that we might discuss the final details about the food for the buffet dinner, the number of bartenders, and when the cake would be delivered. Once more the dreadful odor greeted us!

"I hope it doesn't smell like this when the guests arrive," the lady said nervously.

"That night I watched an episode of *Unsolved Mysteries*. The subject was supernatural odors. The odor accompanying the story was described as resembling the 'odor of dead meat.' When I told some friends they said, 'Ah, that's the ghost of his first wife! She doesn't want the second wife there.' Now I really began to worry. The birthday celebrant was very distinguished and the party guests included a banker, a state senator, and important people from the Mystic Seaport Museum. I could just imagine the good name of the Crary Homestead being ruined by a ghost that smelled worse than a dozen dead skunks!

"On the night of the party the wife set out with her unsuspecting husband for a destination he thought was to be his favorite restaurant. It was located on the same road as we are. Meanwhile everyone was gathering here to honor him at the Crary Homestead. It was almost time for the guest of honor to arrive and fifty or sixty people were here. Now the couple came in, and, to his delighted surprise, he was surrounded by the smiling faces of his friends. All was well.

"Meanwhile, a friend of mine went through the back room to go outside to have a cigarette. The second wife came back to check on things for he saw her through the window. After finishing his cigarette my gentleman friend walked through the same room and experienced an almost electrical jolt of horror. The nauseous odor was back! My friend is a scientist, the head of the biology department at a well-known university and not known for imagining things. He hurriedly aired the room and went back to join the guests. That disaster had been averted by another that was on the way," says Ruth Keyes continuing her story.

"The presents had been opened, and it was time to cut the birthday cake. It was made by a person in town famed for baking excellent cakes. It was his favorite, a lovely, moist carrot cake. Everyone stood in a circle, offering birthday toasts, and waited for his wife to cut it. As she tried to cut the first slice, the entire cake fell apart. Underneath the icing was nothing but a pile of crumbs!"

A sweet revenge?

It would seem that the spirit of the first wife prevailed at last!

Red Brook Inn is a short drive from Old Mystic attractions such as the Mystic Seaport Museum, the Marinelife Aquarium, the Nautilus Memorial, historic sea captains' homes, and two large casinos. The address is P.O. Box 237, Old Mystic, Connecticut 06372 (860–572–0349).

A SHOT IN THE DARK
Hotel del Coronado, Coronado, California

Across from San Diego on a balmy beach by the blue Pacific, is the Hotel del Coronado. It is a legendary place. The Prince of Wales (Edward VIII), Ronald Reagan, Richard Nixon, Lyndon B. Johnson, Marilyn Monroe, John Wayne, Shirley MacLaine, and countless other celebrities have enjoyed its 1880s opulence.

Built when Wyatt Earp was keeping order in Tombstone, the palatial hotel is one of the last great seaside resorts. It has excellent food, a magnificent expanse of ocean, and a haunted room.

The hotel on Orange Avenue in Coronado resembles at first view a huge colony of many different-sized mushrooms, each capped with a pointed red Mediterranean roof. When I went to the desk and inquired about the haunted room, the assistant manager replied abruptly, "We do not have such a thing." I nodded politely and asked to see the manager.

"Well we do have a room that some people say is haunted," answered the manager reluctantly, "but, of course, it isn't."

"Would it be possible for me to see it anyway?"

"No, I'm sorry it wouldn't."

That seemed a strange reply, so I went on to explain that I was collecting stories for a book of supernatural phenomena at famous places. Again, I asked to view the room and again, he refused.

"Would you like to rent it?" he asked.

"What number is it?"

"Number 3502."

How odd that he immediately knew the number if it were not haunted. *Something* must have happened in this room, I thought. "Well, what is the price?"

"It would be one hundred and five dollars."

That seemed reasonable enough for a haunted room, I thought. "Would you kindly show it to me?"

"I'm sorry ma'am, I can't do that, but if you wish to rent it for the night . . ."

"Thank you," I said. "I'll think about it and let you know later," I had another approach in mind, but it could wait. It was time to try the Sunday luncheon buffet in the majestic Crown Room. An impressive display of delicacies graced the long tables, and I observed at least a dozen varieties of luscious-looking desserts. As I sampled the buffet, I admired the dark magnificence of the vaulted oak ceiling, contemplating all the famous people who had dined here. There was a sense of awe at being in the same room where Charles Lindbergh had been honored following his solo flight across the Atlantic in 1927. Here too the Prince of Wales had been feted, and, unfortunately for a man named Simpson, it was on that occasion that his wife, Wallis, met the prince.

But on with the ghost story quest. After brunch, questioning various employees of the hotel, I discovered that many had heard stories of the room being haunted and some believed them.

Through the years the girl's identity and details of her background gradually came to light. The true story is not a happy one. It is about a wicked stepmother and a lovely young girl.

Kate Morgan was born in Dubuque, Iowa, three years after the close of the Civil War. Her father was a well-to-do farmer, and, when she was a child, he and her mother gave the golden-haired little Kate every advantage. She was in her early teens when her

The legendary Hotel del Coronado near San Diego has a room said to be haunted.

mother died and her father remarried. Despite the girl's efforts to please her stepmother, Maggie, she was never able to do so, and as time went on, the girl's life became increasingly miserable.

The lovely clothes her parents had given her were now tattered and outgrown, and anything Morgan did for his daughter made her stepmother madly jealous. Even his bringing her a bright ribbon from the store was an occasion for harsh words from his wife. It irritated Maggie that despite Kate's faded calico dresses her beauty shone bright as a new Indian head penny.

In 1868 Dubuque showed some of the promise and much of the tawdry glitter of the city it would one day become. Rough bootclad cattlemen trod the muddy streets, their pockets full of money to squander, and saloons and gambling houses attracted all kinds of men.

Demure, well-dressed ladies flourished parasols shielding their delicate complexions from the rays of the blazing Midwest sun as they strolled along the wooden sidewalk in front of the stores. And then there were women whose hair boasted a brassy henna brilliance and who wore color on their lips as red as the blossoms of the trumpet vines that twined over unpainted shacks. Real ladies could spot that kind in a twinkling, Maggie Morgan always said, and with her sharp tongue was ever ready to point them out contemptuously.

Often while Maggie lay languidly in bed resting, Kate was sent through the flat Iowa countryside, bright with purple phlox and wild roses, on errands to the store. One July afternoon she had just come out of the Dubuque Supply Company, carrying her purchases when a cattleman grasped her arm.

"You're sure a pretty gal. I wanna buy you a drink," Bill Bailey said.

Kate pulled away and tried to pass him, but his big, calloused hand reached out, encircling her waist, and he spun her around to face him.

"Please, let me go. I don't know you, sir."

"Wal, you can git to know me mighty fast!" With that, he jerked Kate toward him, and her bag full of groceries fell from her arms, its contents spilling all over the ground.

"I seen you before, wearin' them raggedy clothes. You need a purty dress, a gal like you." He thrust his bearded face close to Kate's own. She screamed, and a knot of men began to gather around them. Kate strained to break free, and, as she did, her dress tore at the shoulder. She began to cry.

"Now, see what you went and done," Bill said, leering at her. "I tole you, you needed a purty dress, and I'm going to take you to git it."

"You're not taking her anywhere," a hard-edged masculine

voice spoke up from the crowd. Bill Bailey glared at the man the crowd parted to let pass. A tall, well-built fellow with bright blue eyes, curly black hair, and expensive clothes, it was obvious he was no cattleman.

Bailey released Kate and, fists raised, started for the stranger but stopped abruptly when the man's hand slid toward his pocket. That meant a pistol. Bailey turned away, melting into the little knot of onlookers. The stranger covered Kate's bare shoulder by putting his jacket around her and began picking up the contents of her bag from the dirt of the main street.

"I want to see you safely home," he said. "What is your name, young lady?"

"Kate Morgan. And yours, sir?"

"Lou Garrou."

She rode behind him on his horse, and Garrou seemed in no hurry. He had gotten off a Mississippi riverboat that afternoon and was in town to enjoy himself. In answer to her question about his occupation, he said, "Just a traveling businessman," and that he would be moving on in a day or so. He came back to see her that night and the following afternoon, much to everyone's astonishment, he appeared at the Morgan farmhouse with a box of pretty clothes for Kate. Since he was still there at suppertime, they invited him to sit down and share their meal.

When Garrou showed up about noon on the third day, he asked Kate's father if he could marry her. The surprised farmer told Garrou that he didn't know as to how his daughter should marry a traveling man.

"Well it's time I settled down on some land of my own," Lou replied, chewing thoughtfully on a blade of grass. Kate's father liked the sound of that, and her stepmother, eager to get rid of the girl, said, "It's high time Kate got married."

So a justice of the peace performed the ceremony, and afterward

Morgan pressed a fifty-dollar note into his daughter's hand. It was the first time since her mother's death that Kate had seen tears in his eyes.

The river looked like a sheet of gold in the late afternoon sun as the couple boarded a Mississippi packet heading south to Savannah, Fulton, Comanche, and Moline. The names all sounded exciting to Kate. But while the big paddles of the boat rhythmically pounded the water, Kate found out what her husband's "business" was. He was a gambler.

That night she cried and told him he had deceived her. He became angry and asked her what difference his making a living gambling made if she cared about him, and, if she didn't, she could always go home. Kate could just imagine the anger in her step-mother's face if she showed up at the front door. There was nothing to do but make the best of it.

From then on Lou and Kate traveled everywhere there were gambling tables and card games. When they were not on riverboats, they stayed in cities like San Francisco or Sacramento, anywhere Lou could find games with high enough stakes. Usually, he registered Kate under the name Mrs. Anderson Barnard. Whether this was his real name or one he had chosen to protect his identity if there was trouble he would never say. But Kate did know that after the card games there were sometimes hot words and angry losers.

In a few years she settled in Visalia, California, while Lou went on traveling. Sometimes he would show up unexpectedly, promise her he was going to change, stay for a week or two and then leave again. During one of these visits, Kate said, "Why can't we live like other people do."

"You're right, honey. We'll buy us a little house in Los Angeles and start a family," he said, hugging her.

They bought the house he had promised and for a while Lou

seemed content. Because he was, so was Kate. There were games around town, and money rolled in. Lou tried hard not to become too greedy. He would win a few games, then let himself lose one or two, keeping his bets small. But after four or five months of this, he began to get restless. It was just like it had always been when they stayed anywhere for long. The stakes in the games weren't big enough, or there was more money to be made elsewhere—Frisco or Denver. Then one night he didn't come home. He had never done that before or left town without telling her. That was the first of October of 1892, and a few weeks later Kate found that she was pregnant. She wanted to tell Lou, but where was he?

Just before Thanksgiving a letter arrived. He wrote that he didn't think he would ever be able to settle down, and it wasn't right for a pretty woman like her to be saddled with a drifter. He would see her in a few weeks and bring the money for her to get a divorce. "You keep the house," he wrote. "A man like me has got no use for one."

Kate was heartbroken, but sure that when he found out about the baby, everything would change, she would find him. One of his favorite haunts was the Hotel del Coronado in San Diego. There was all the money she had saved for an emergency under the fancy black-and-gold French clock he had once given her. The next day she bought some lovely new clothes with part of it. She would go to San Diego and join him. He would be happy over her news. Everything would be the way it was during the early years, except that now there would be the three of them.

When she arrived at the Hotel del Coronado, she registered as Mrs. Lottie Anderson Barnard. She could scarcely wait to dress and go to the game room. When she did arrive and look in the door, there sat Lou playing cards at one of the tables. A pretty woman, her arms looped affectionately around his neck, leaned over him as he played. Kate saw him lay his cards on the table, smiling triumphantly, and reach up to touch the woman's arm. You might have heard a heart break, you might have heard a tear drop, if it were possible to hear either.

Lou did not look toward the doorway and Kate never entered the room. Turning quickly away, she walked through the vast lobby out to one of the carriages sitting in front of the hotel and gave the driver the address of a shop in San Diego. When the carriage brought her back to the hotel she was carrying a paper bag.

Back in room 302, Kate unfolded the pretty clothes she had bought the day before she left Los Angeles, threw them in the fireplace, and touched the newspaper beneath the kindling with one of the large wooden matches from the small white china match box on the mantel. Then she took from her suitcase a bracelet of woven hair with a picture of a man's face set in the medallion's centerpiece, looked at it, and threw it into the fire on top of the clothing. Last to go into the flames was her pocketbook.

Picking up the paper bag, Kate started down the long carpeted hallway to the elevator. The door of the ornate brass cage closed behind her. Was there anything else she should do? Yes, one more thing.

"Is a Mr. Lou Garrou registered here?" she asked, stopping at the desk.

The clerk went through the cards on the rack. "Yes, madam. Through Sunday."

"May I have a piece of paper?" Kate wrote three sentences on it. *Lottie Barnard was registered in room 302. She loved you very much. She came to tell you your child was on the way.*

"Would you have someone take this note to him in the game room in about fifteen minutes?"

"Of course, madam."

It was raining heavily when Kate went out the hotel door leading to the oceanfront veranda. She heard the angry rumble of thunder and paused for a moment as flashes of lightning illuminated the scene. Then she reached into the paper bag and, withdrawing the .44 pistol, placed the barrel against her right temple and fired. Muffled by the crashing dissonance of the storm, the shot went unheard. An early riser found her rain-soaked body the next morning and a crowd of shocked guests gathered on the veranda. Whether a gambler who called himself Lou Garrou was among them will never be known.

Opinions of the hotel staff vary from denials that anything ever happened here to admitting nervousness when they must enter the room that was once 302 and today is room 3502. An examination of the floor plan of the hotel in 1892 reveals that this was once a larger room with a cozy fireplace made smaller to accommodate the present built-in bathroom.

One of the elevator operators was more communicative than some other members of the staff. He said guests had questioned him about eerie lights flickering outside 3502. Once a gentleman said he had encountered a young woman in an old-fashioned dress and coat standing, soaked to the bone, at the door of the room late at night. He told of maids hearing the sound of weeping inside. The next morning when they unlocked the door to clean, the room had not been occupied.

Over the years the stories persist. Stormy nights especially give rise to them. Does poor Kate still return to weep over her gambler husband and unborn child?

There is no resort hotel on either coast that can quite match the Hotel del Coronado, which is a National Historic Landmark. Whether you rent room 3502 or not, a stay in this seaside palace is unforgettable. For reservations or information, write to the Hotel del Coronado, 1500 Orange Avenue, Coronado, California 92118, or telephone (619) 435–6611.

RETURN OF
THE HANGED MAN

Whaley House (Museum), San Diego, California

The Whaley House in San Diego is one of only two houses in California that the United States Chamber of Commerce has authenticated as being genuinely haunted. What does "genuinely haunted" mean? We must visit Old Town to find out.

June Reading, a graduate of the University of Minnesota, is curator and chief historian of this house. She undoubtedly has done more research and knows more than anyone else in the world about the family who built it. Located north of downtown San Diego, it is a historic site that people come to visit from all over the world. No members of the Whaley family inhabit the house—at least none that are still alive.

Whaley House has been written about in many publications, and if you have been wondering as you read these stories what makes a house haunted, a description by D. Scott Rogo, author of *In Search of the Unknown*, is enlightening. It seems to describe this house perfectly.

Rogo says that what is necessary are apparitions, unaccountable cold feelings or sensations of being touched by something intangible, and other phenomena such as lights, footsteps, rappings, movements of objects, unaccountable odors, and presences.

According to June Reading, Whaley House has exhibited every one of these phenomena and more since 1960, the year it was opened to the public, and "the manifestations are still going on."

Mrs. Reading was active in the restoration of the house from the very beginning. The first events she remembers occurred during the early work. I found myself alert for any sound later as I stood beside her and listened in the narrow downstairs hall.

"One day in the spring of 1960, I had come over here early, intending to see about furnishing the upstairs rooms. Two staff members from the San Diego Historical Society were loaned to me to help with the delivery of the furniture and other items. As I walked to the back door, they followed. When I reached up to unbolt the door, we clearly heard the sound of walking across the upper floor. My companions insisted that someone else was in the house, so I mounted the stairs and called out, hoping to get a response. There was no reply.

"As I turned to come down, saying 'There's no one upstairs,' we both looked at each other and said, 'Well, maybe Thomas Whaley's come back to look the place over!'

"Suddenly we heard the sound of footsteps coming from the bedroom above us, as if someone were walking in heavy boots. 'Who is upstairs?' asked one of the men. I shook my head, and he laughed about spirits coming back to look things over, and I thought no more about it." Mrs. Reading and I walked up the stairs together as she continued her story. "At the time I thought another workman had arrived ahead of us, but later when I came to see, no one was up here.

"At first we were so busy getting the place ready for the public that I was really unaware of unusual sounds in the old house. But in the days after it was opened, I would often hear the same footsteps and find myself going upstairs again and again, sure that someone must be up there. Sometimes it happened when I was busy at my

Supernatural happenings are not "out of the ordinary" at the Whaley House, San Diego's oldest home. It is one of two houses that the state has authenticated as haunted.

desk downstairs or when visitors were on the lower floor. I would sit at my desk and hear heavy feet descend the hall stairs, but for some reason they always stopped about three steps from the bottom.

"One morning in October of 1962, I was giving a talk to twenty-five school children who were touring the house. This time the sound of footsteps began to come from on top of the flat roof. The school children began to look up at the ceiling curiously and ask me, 'Who is making that noise?' so I went outside expecting to see a repairman sent by the county. No one was up there. When I mentioned some of these events to people in the neighborhood, they said "That sort of phenomenon has gone on for years.'"

The last member of the family to live in the house was Lillian Whaley. She was well aware that unusual things went on there, and, during the many years she lived in the house, she had often complained about them. On one occasion she even told of a heavy china cabinet that suddenly toppled over without cause. That was in 1912, one year before Frank Whaley's death. Lillian Whaley lived in Whaley House all her life and was the only child who did not marry. She was eighty-nine when she died in 1953.

On one occasion while Mrs. Reading was guiding a tour, a woman visitor complained that she had felt unseen hands pushing her out of an upstairs bedroom. And many have mentioned smelling cologne, rose water, or the aroma of cigar smoke when they have been alone in one of the rooms.

One such tourist, Mrs. Kirby, wife of the director of the Medical Association of New Westminster, British Columbia, was convinced that she had seen the apparition of a woman in the house's courtroom. Mrs. Kirby described a small, olive-skinned lady in a bright calico dress with a full skirt down to the floor who simply "stared right through me."

One of the ghosts who, I am told, has been seen in the house with regularity is Squire Augustus S. Ensworth. Ensworth was an attorney who managed Thomas Whaley's business enterprises in San Diego while Whaley was in the Quartermaster Department in San Francisco during the Civil War. He was very fond of the Whaley House and took great pride in keeping it in good repair during Mr. Whaley's absence. Augustus Ensworth's spirit is said to still hover protectively around Whaley House.

Mrs. Anna Whaley is presumably responsible for the occasional snatches of piano music. And then there are evidences of the playful spirit of little Tom Whaley, who died in one of the upstairs rooms when he was only seventeen months old.

"An event occurred just before Christmas," recalls Mrs. Reading "when several of us were in the old courtroom getting popcorn and cranberry ropes and other old-fashioned ornaments ready for the tree. One of the hostesses very quietly went around to get a good view and shot a picture of all of us. After the film had been sent off and developed, she brought in the prints. To her own and everyone else's amazement, over at the edge of the group stood a woman in a period dress. The resemblance to Mrs. Whaley was striking."

The eerie things that have happened to guides in the house and to tourists as well do not occur every day. Sometimes weeks go by and nothing out of the ordinary occurs—nothing, that is, that would send chills down one's spine or cause one to shiver on a warm day. But then something will take place that no one can explain. June Reading tells the story of such an event.

"In the early 1980s a lovely college girl named Denise Pournelle worked at the house during the summer, and, from the moment she arrived, she went around telling everyone how she would love to see a ghost. Things like this can be dangerous to say, particularly in certain houses where even the walls may be listening. I always thought it was like tempting Providence, but Denise kept right on. I talked with her and advised her to be patient.

"'Denise, sooner or later you are going to hear wailing, you are going to hear music, and you'll even get the feeling that someone is touching you. You will have all kinds of things happen to you.' Of course, I was right.

"It was during Christmas vacation and she was like a child loving to dress up in costume. We always do that here at the house on special occasions. That afternoon we were all in our old-fashioned long dresses and there was a cold rain most of the day, so we had very few visitors except for one little boy. This boy walked all over the house trying to hear the sound of a ghost. He also sat on the stairs, thinking that, if he concentrated, he might hear footsteps. The kids that come here are so cute. I remember him because he had a pair of tennis shoes on that were unusually clean.

"The hostesses were sitting around because there was so little activity. I hadn't eaten anything, and it was getting into the afternoon, so I told them I was going out to have a late lunch. When I came back, they were all waiting for me at the front door. Before I could even get my coat off, they said, 'While you were gone, we heard the footsteps upstairs, not once but twice. There was a long pause, and then they started again.'

"Denise's dark eyes were sparkling, and her pretty face was filled with excitement, so I said, 'Denise, why don't you come upstairs with me? I'm a little suspicious.' I had that little boy with the tennis shoes on my mind instead of any ghost, because that child could have slipped away from the ladies without their noticing it and gone upstairs into one of the rooms.

"Denise picked up her long skirt, and up we went. The first place we walked into was the master bedroom, and two windows were standing wide open. It was pouring rain, the rain had come in and was all over the floor, and the curtains were dripping wet. I was angry and said to myself, do you suppose that boy came up here, opened those windows and prowled around?

"Together, we looked in the other rooms but could see no evidence that anyone had been in them. The rain was so bad that it was almost dark out, although it was only about two-thirty in the afternoon. So I began to close the windows, but the frames are all the original white cedar that swells up just like a sponge when it gets wet. They were so swollen that I could hardly close them, and I certainly don't know how anyone could have pulled them open.

"I could not get them bolted, and I said, 'Denise, you are going to have to go downstairs and get a hammer.' She said, 'Let me try it,' and together we finally got the bolt over. Then we walked into the nursery and, once there, began to relax because nothing was out of place. Suddenly, just a few feet behind us, a man's deep laugh rang out. Denise said, 'Did you hear that?' I said, 'What did you hear?' She said, 'I heard a man's laughter.' I said, 'So did I!'

" 'Let's get out of here!' Denise cried, and with that, she picked up her skirts and down the stairs she went—lickety split. She dashed over to the telephone and called her mother. I knew that we had both heard laughter from the past. I felt what I can only describe as an intense electric shock go the length of my back, and for a few seconds I stood there frozen, truly unable to move. I have never had anything affect me in such a way.

"As for Denise, her face was white and her eyes were terrified. I would never have imagined we could get down the stairs so fast in long dresses. It is a wonder we didn't break our necks. I don't recall Denise ever mentioning any desire for a supernatural experience again.

"After we began to talk about it downstairs, I remembered that the place where we had been standing when we heard the laugh was right over the location of the old gallows that stood there before Thomas Whaley built this house. He had watched the hanging of a colorful man named Yankee Jim. Imprisoned for attempting to steal a boat, Yankee Jim's crime does not seem as grave as the sort for which men were ordinarily sentenced to hang. Unfortunately for him, his trial came upon the heels of the Indian uprising of 1851, when San Diego had been under martial law and any sort of disorder occasioned swift and sometimes harsh action.

"Yankee Jim did not take the sentence of hanging him seriously, and, believing he would be pardoned at the last minute, even made jokes on his way to the gallows. But he was not pardoned. His last moments were painful, indeed, for when the wagon in which he was standing was pulled from under his feet, his neck remained unbroken. He continued to live for almost an hour, until he finally strangled to death."

Is it possible that the laugh they heard that afternoon was Yankee Jim? "It may be," admitted Mrs. Reading. "I sometimes wonder if certain sounds remain forever in the atmosphere, or perhaps accessible, and now and then something we do sets them off. Then we hear that sound again exactly as it once occurred. The footsteps, the laugh, even the old-fashioned melodies we occasionally hear playing in the music room of the house . . . Thomas Whaley once wrote in a letter to his mother, 'My wife is the best little woman in the world, loved by all, she is proficient in music, plays and sings.' Perhaps she is still heard here.

"I could tell you many other strange things," continued June Reading, "but the sound of that deep laugh shocked me more than anything else that has ever happened to me in this house."

For those who are fascinated by ghost stories, it is said that four different ghosts have been identified at the Whaley House. The most noisy of all is reputed to be that of Yankee Jim.

Whatever your tastes, you are welcome to enjoy a tour of this early home of the Old West. Located at 2482 San Diego Avenue in Old Town, San Diego, California, Whaley House, with its rich and violent chronicles of yesteryear, is now open to the public Wednesday through Sunday year-round. For more information, telephone (619) 298-2482. For those who suffer from the summer heat elsewhere, the cool breezes off the bay and temperatures during the day ranging between 65 and 75 degrees are delightful. Bring a sweater for evenings outdoors.

THE HOUSE THE SPIRITS BUILT

The Winchester Mansion, San Jose, California

A luxurious black carriage cruised slowly through one of Boston's old neighborhoods, along a once fashionable street lined with what were once grand houses. Now paint peeled from most of them, and soot from coal-burning furnaces gave the neighborhood a bedraggled look. The driver peered at the front of each building, trying to make out the numbers. He stopped before a dirty mustard-colored house with cream trim.

Standing nervously on the porch, he turned an etched, brass doorbell, which made a jarring, metallic sound. How strange to make a trip to this neighborhood just a day after the great man's funeral. Whatever could Mrs. Winchester and her niece expect to find here? He waited. Would anyone answer?

Suddenly the knob turned and the door opened. The driver stepped back, startled. On the threshold stood a tall woman with deep-set, olive-colored eyes. Her pasty white face was shaped like a hatchet and her black hair, pulled back severely, was wound in an immense twist on top of her head. She wore a long, somewhat shabby brown dress and an ancient shawl. The driver's usually impassive face must have reflected shock, for the woman looked at him harshly and then glanced at the fashionable carriage in front of the house.

"She will have to come in, you know. Go tell her that Mrs. Raven is ready to see her."

He went back to the brougham, opened the back door, and relayed the message just as it had been given him. A gloved hand emerged and rested upon his arm as he helped a tiny, heavily veiled woman in black from the carriage. She was followed by a younger lady, wearing a hat with a soft veil wound about its brim. The driver, Charles Farnham, accompanied them to the front door, where the older woman made a peremptory motion for him to return to the carriage. When he looked back, the pair had disappeared into the house.

Farnham was uneasy. It was not just that the expensive brougham was attracting attention in an unsavory neighborhood; it was the appearance of the woman who had opened the door. There was something evil about her. More than an hour passed, and his two passengers were still inside the house. He was tempted to go up and ring the bell to be certain that they were all right, but he didn't really dare, not yet. Restlessly he pulled out a cigarette. What were they doing inside that house all this time? He watched a fine, light drizzle of rain beginning to spatter the shiny black of the carriage.

It was getting dark and still the lights hadn't gone on inside. Why didn't the Raven woman light a lamp? He had almost gathered up his courage to check and see if madam and her niece were all right when the front door opened. Miss Margaret came out first and her aunt, Sarah Winchester, followed. Mrs. Winchester turned back toward the darkness of the doorway to speak to someone he assumed was Mrs. Raven. Since the death of William Wirt Winchester, son of Oliver Winchester, the "rifle king," Mrs. Winchester's sole companion had been Margaret.

This was the first of many trips Farnham was to make during the winter of 1884 from the Winchester mansion at Hartford, Connecticut, to the shabby street in Boston. Sometimes Margaret would accompany her aunt; on other occasions Sarah Pardee Winchester would go alone. She never seemed herself after a trip to the Witch's Palace, as Farnham had begun to call the mustard-colored house in his own mind. After the last visit, Mrs. Winchester appeared extremely frightened. She clutched Margaret's arm and talked hysterically.

"Do you know what she says, Margaret? She says the money William left me has a curse on it!"

"Why would she say that?"

"She says the spirits of all those men and women that were killed by the Winchester are haunting my fortune and that they mean to harm me."

"But there were lots of people killed by the rifle," Margaret protested reasonably. "Soldiers, Indians . . ."

"Oh! Don't say the word *Indians*. According to Mrs. Raven they will be the worst haunters, and there is just one way to keep them from getting me!"

"And what way is that, Auntie?"

"She says it can be done only by my getting a larger house that will attract good spirits. The good spirits will keep the evil ones away and the house must be fixed up according to their wishes."

"But how will you know their wishes, Auntie?"

"Mrs. Raven will guide me as to what to do."

Farnham, who was doing his best to hear the conversation, shook his head. People said her husband had left her twenty million dollars. It was hard for him even to imagine how much money that was. But despite her wealth, he had begun to feel sorry for Mrs. Winchester. Poor woman, the death of her husband must have affected her mind.

It could be a nightmare to find one's way out of the Winchester House, particularly for the terrified young girl in this story.

On their last trip to the house in Boston, just as they were about to get into the carraige, something huge and white flew past them and Mrs. Winchester screamed. Farnham thought it could have been a large owl startled by their lights, and he and Margaret tried to soothe Sarah Winchester. She almost collapsed in front of Mrs. Raven's house, and it took his and her niece's combined efforts to get her into the back seat of the carriage.

The next day, to everyone's surprise, Mrs. Winchester announced that she was moving to California. Farnham overheard her tell Miss Margaret that she believed the owl had been a warning to her that they must leave Hartford immediately. "From now on, the spirits themselves will lead me." Of the staff given the opportunity to move, none accepted but Farnham, who was unmarried at the time.

Once in San Jose, Sarah Winchester bought an eighteen-room house. Her first move was to hire twenty-two carpenters to immediately commence adding a wing to the house. Landscape gardeners were the next to arrive and they began to plant a towering hedge that shut off any view of the house from the road. Then seven Japanese gardeners were hired to fertilize and prune the hedge so that no one could possibly see through it.

Before they had left Hartford, Mrs. Winchester used to talk with Farnham occasionally. Now she never spoke to him or to any of the other servants. All instructions for everyone had to come through Miss Margaret, her niece and secretary. The veil Mrs. Winchester put on for mourning was never removed except in the presence of the Chinese butler who served her dinner. Farnham began to find that he could scarcely remember Mrs. Winchester's features. Once, years later, Farnham asked Won Lee what Mrs. Winchester looked like now.

"She little old lady," replied the butler, shrugging. "Look like shriveled plum."

From the time of her arrival in the San Jose house, carpenters and masons were at work seven days a week. There seemed to be no hurry about completing many of the projects, and the workmen wondered why they were asked to be there on Sundays, holidays, and even Christmas Day. They had no idea of the warning a Boston spiritualist had given Mrs. Winchester.

"As long as hammers ring out day and night, nothing bad will ever happen to you. Only then will the good spirits keep the bad spirits away." And so the hammers continued to ring out.

Sarah Winchester was holding séances alone now in the séance room, sitting for hours with her pen poised to write down the spirits' instructions for her life. The message she believed she was receiving through Mrs. Raven was that *she must accomplish two tasks.* The first was to keep out low and depraved spirits who would try their utmost to harm her. The second was to please the good spirits whom she would one day join when she moved on to the next world. Both tasks were very expensive. The good spirits could be pleased only by the most lavish furnishings and therefore every room had to be furnished like a royal palace.

It was vital that none of the evil spirits should ever get into the small, bare-walled séance room, which no living person but she could enter until after her death. If anyone did, they might contain a depraved spirit that could contaminate the room and prevent her from reaching "heaven". Therefore her way of getting to the séance room was a secret one through a labyrinth of passages and rooms. To elude and frustrate the evil spirits whom she believed sought to follow her, she spent hours planning unusual and unexpected construction tricks for the carpenters to execute.

Once these tricks were completed, she could, for example, push a button, that would make a wall panel recede, and she could step swiftly from one apartment to another. Then she could open a window and climb out, not onto a roof, but to the top of a flight of steps that would take her down one story to meet another flight that would bring her back up to the original level. The theory was that this maze of stairs would trick and confuse the spirits of the Indian ghosts.

In addition to stairs that led nowhere, she had the carpenters build a huge room full of nothing but balconies. These balconies were of all sorts and sizes. Here the bewildered spirit might dash around a corner only to find that a balcony had suddenly shrunk from being three feet wide and was now only three inches! One balcony led to a door that, once closed, would not open from inside. Mrs. Winchester believed this would force the spirit to find another escape route. Of course everything was only temporary, a way to delay for a few minutes the evil spirits that hurried after her.

After at least half an hour of maneuvering to be certain that she had eluded her last ghostly pursuer, Mrs. Winchester would arrive at last in front of a piece of furniture resembling a large wardrobe with drawers in the bottom of it. But like almost everything else in Sarah Winchester's house, it was just another deception, for one door was not a wardrobe door at all. It really led into the séance room. Once through this door, she would emerge safely into the secret room on the other side of the wall, finally attaining her objective. The walls were painted blue, for it is widely believed among superstitious people that this color frightens away evil spirits. In the room was a cabinet, a comfortable armchair, and, in front of the latter, a table with paper and pencil for automatic writing and a planchette board to receive the spirit messages. There are spots on the floor of this room where the varnish has been worn away by the constant tread of her slippers.

Today, there are few people left alive who remember Sarah Winchester. But one of those who does is Maria. Now an old woman herself, she still shivers about an experience she had as a girl when she worked in the Winchester house.

It all started quite accidentally. Maria had been employed there for only a month and was hurrying to leave to prepare for a date that night with her young man. She took a wrong turn as she left the wing of the house in which she worked, and within minutes she was hopelessly lost in the labyrinth of connecting passages between the (by then) almost 150 rooms.

At one point she was sure she was near one of the passages to the outside world; instead, Maria found herself on a stairway with seven separate flights. Breathless, she reached a door and managed to open it, only to find that the wall behind it was solid. Panic stricken, she attempted to retrace her steps but discovered she was on a sunporch that she had never seen—and it had a skylight in the floor! The next room she entered was also unfamiliar. She turned to go back out, only to realize in a panic that the door to this room did not open from the inside. Finally she found another way out.

Her experience was assuming all the qualities of a nightmare, except that it was real. She walked along a balcony and, seeing an open window, stepped through it; but in a moment she found that she was back on another part of the same balcony. By now she was hysterical. On she hurried up one flight of steps and down another.

Finally she opened a door and stumbled into a small, windowless cell of a room. There, seated at a table, was a little old lady glaring at her with an expression of unspeakable rage. It was Mrs. Winchester. "You have disturbed the spirits," she shouted.

Maria had never really seen her employer, for she was always heavily veiled, and all the servants knew that no one was ever permitted to see her face. The combination of the forbidden sight and the anger she saw there caused the poor girl to faint. The ending of this story is told in Maria's own words.

"When I woke up, I was lying on a bed in the servants' quarters and within minutes was hustled out of the house and driven home. When I got out, the chauffeur gave me an envelope and told me I was never to come to work again. In the envelope there was my notice from Miss Margaret and six months' salary. Even if I had not been fired, I could not have returned to that house."

Are there ghosts or spirits in the Winchester house?

"I really don't know. But one thing I'm sure of is that the medium who said Mrs. Winchester's fortune was haunted by spirits that would harm her was evil. She took advantage of a woman's grief after the death of her husband and told her lies that destroyed her."

For the rest of her life all Mrs. Winchester's energy and money was spent on ways to protect herself from her strange imaginings.

Mrs. Winchester was convinced by a spiritualist medium that the lives of her husband and baby daughter had been taken by spirits of those killed by the Gun That Won the West. She, too, would share their fate unless she never stopped building a mansion for the spirits. She would live only for as long as she continued to build. She built for almost thirty-eight years. The lavish, 160-room mansion, with forty-seven fireplaces, thirteen bathrooms, and endless spiritualistic symbols sprawls over six acres and is a California Historical Landmark. Located at 525 South Winchester Boulevard in San Jose, the house is open daily for tours except on Christmas Day. For more information, telephone (408) 247–2101.

This story is a work of fiction. Names, characters, and events are purely fictitious and a product of the author's imagination. In no way does this story reflect on the present fine management of the Winchester Mystery House, which has been offering guided tours of this unique mansion on a daily basis since 1923.

THE THING IN THE WELL

Old Fort Niagara, Youngstown, New York

When the moon is full above the Castle on a summer night—that is when they say it happens. And for all we know, it may be happening tonight. Pray it won't. Or pray, at least, that neither you nor I will be there to see it if it should.

But wait—in my horror, I am getting ahead of myself.

Old Fort Niagara at Youngstown, New York, is one of the northernmost historic sites in the United States. The impressive French Castle, as it is called, was erected in 1726. These fortifications, which guarded the vital water route to the West and were occupied at various times by French voyagers, British grenadiers, and American soldiers, have been well preserved. Today the Castle is just as it stood before the Revolution, with its massive stone walls and bastions, blockhouses and stockade, moat and drawbridge. In the summer months the roar of muskets and roll of drums reverberate beside Lake Ontario as colorful pageantry celebrates the history of the old fortifications.

Most military forts have seen both good and evil days. Just as the body of a murdered man sometimes rises to the surface of the water to expose his murderer, dark deeds that once took place here persist among the legends surrounding Old Fort Niagara. One grisly event continues to be told. Our story begins in the days just before the Indian War, when two French soldiers, whom we shall call Henri Le Clerc and Jean-Claude de Rochefort, were stationed here. The fort in which they lived was a little city in itself, the largest place south of Montreal or west of Albany. Everything that the soldiers needed for daily life was here. They had a mess hall, barracks, bakery, blacksmith shop, and, for worship, a small chapel with a large, ancient dial over the door to mark the hourly course of the sun.

The well in the center of the Castle was there in the event the fort was ever surrounded and besieged. After the British captured and occupied it in 1759, they feared the French might have poisoned the water. So they filled the well with dirt and covered the top with large, flat stones that matched the rest of the floor. It was not until the 1920s that the well was restored.

In those early years a burial ground lay just outside the massive gates, and over its entrance was painted, in large characters, the word REST. Just how some of the poor wretches were sent to their "rest" in this barren field is open to speculation. Undoubtedly, there were those who came straight from the dungeon to the burial ground, for this fort also served as a harsh prison.

The dungeon was called the Black Hole. It was a dark and dismal place. Over in one corner was a barbarous apparatus used for strangling those who offended the despotic rulers of a time when both justice and mercy were in short supply. On the dungeon's walls, from top to bottom, prisoners had laboriously carved their names, a few pitiful words, or a family emblem.

Imagine the distress of one merchant at the fort who decided to hide some valuables in the dungeon when an attack was expected by superior British forces. He went there late one night and, on the wall, from among hundreds of French names, one leaped out at him. It was his own family name, d'Artagnan, carved in large letters.

Once, the bones of a woman were found when it became necessary to clear out an old mess-hall sink, confirming people's suspi-

One of the many legends that surround Old Fort Niagara is an old and grisly story about this building, the French Castle.

cions that the fort was often the scene of foul murder. Thus, amid the natural beauty of the land and the lake, it is clear that the most atrocious crimes also took place in Old Fort Niagara. But let us return to our story.

During any occupation, there is a need for celebrations to break the monotony, and the French often held parties on the third floor of the Castle. It was the custom of the officers to invite a number of Indian girls from the nearby Seneca village. Among the Senecas, women had considerable power and were respected. They both nominated members of the tribal council and removed them if they misbehaved.

Henri Le Clerc, a young man of a good family from Bordeaux, France, had left early on the evening of the party with several fellow officers to escort the women to the Castle. Henri had personal reasons for going, as his heart had been captured by a lovely Indian girl named Onita. They had no sooner arrived at the Seneca village, however, than a cloudburst occurred, and no one wanted to leave until it was over. On the return to the Castle, the sky was clear and the night was beautiful, complete with an enormous full moon. Henri and Onita lingered a little behind the others admiring the moon and happy in each other's company. By the time the girls and their escorts reached the Castle, the wine was flowing freely, for Henri could hear loud talk and outbursts of laughter as they mounted the stairs to the third floor.

"The party is already quite noisy," remarked Onita. Henri agreed. "If some of the men begin to get out of hand, I'll take you back to the village early," he said.

When the girls entered the room, cheers rang out; for a time there was singing and dancing, and all went well. Unfortunately, an officer named Jean-Claude de Rochefort, whom Henri particularly despised, had pulled up a chair and seated himself on the other side of Onita. Jean-Claude was a former seaman, and if he had not once been a pirate, Henri was certain he was at least a scoundrel. Jean-Claude also fancied himself irresistible to the ladies. All efforts that Henri and Onita made at conversation were futile, for Jean-Claude constantly interrupted.

With more wine, his behavior worsened. Several times Onita shook de Rochefort's hand from her arm, but he continued to become even bolder. "Mon petit chou, why do you resist me?" he said, placing his arm around her shoulders and attempting to pull her close.

"Because you are a pig!" the angry young woman shot back at him.

"Why, you little . . . ," shouted Jean-Claude, seizing her roughly and thrusting his face close to hers.

Henri jumped from his chair and struck Jean-Claude's face such a blow that he released the girl in surprise. There was the thud of fists striking flesh and bone. Jean-Claude was getting much the worst of it. He leaped behind a chair and, to the other officers' surprise, drew his sword. Henri had to retreat enough to draw his own weapon.

Henri thrust repeatedly at his attacker, and the greater amount of wine that Jean-Claude had consumed was now giving Henri the advantage. The blade of Henri's sword nicked de Rochefort's arm, then his cheek. Other officers at first tried to stop them but then assumed that the duel would end when one or the other was wounded. Jean-Claude was always volatile, but tonight his temper, combined with alcohol and the insult to his pride, had sent him into a frenzy. Henri had the skill and ability to outlast his foe, however, and the other officers knew it. He withstood the mighty, slashing blows that deflected his skillful thrusts and avoided return lunges by stepping from one side to another to tire his enemy.

Henri moved to keep from backing into one of the Indian girls, and then he realized his danger: He was directly in front of the stairway. Seizing his advantage, Jean-Claude lunged forward with a quick thrust to the body, and involuntarily, Henri stepped back to the brink of the top stair. Now Henri's peril was great, and Jean-Claude became even more reckless. He took a cut across the chin but charged forward with his body like a bull, as if to grab Henri about the waist and hurl him down the stairs. Jean-Claude was a brute of a man, and to avoid grappling with him, Henri moved backward down the stairs.

His only hope was to keep Jean-Claude at a safe distance with the rapier-sharp point of his sword and try for a mortal thrust to the fellow's heart or abdomen. To this end, he slowly retreated down the stairs, waiting for the right moment to deliver the blow. As it seemed that the duel would be a long one, the other officers stayed on the third floor with the Indian girls. The duelists continued down the flight of steps until they were a short distance from the first floor. Henri then began to formulate a more charitable plan: Being the more agile man, when both reached the first floor he would whirl around, mount a few steps, and leap upon Jean-Claude, pinning him to the floor. If he could execute the move quickly enough, he was sure his opponent would admit defeat.

But as Henri's foot reached the third step from the bottom, he tripped and lost his balance. His head struck the stone floor, and all went black. In a moment of insane anger, Jean-Claude raised his sword arm and ran the helpless man through.

A little sanity, or at least the need for self-preservation, then began to return to Jean-Claude de Rochefort. He had committed murder, a deed for which he could hang. Before his crime was discovered, he must somehow get rid of the body. Henri was by no means a small man and would be too heavy to carry. Besides, Jean-Claude had only a short time to dispose of the evidence. What was he to do? He decided to dismember the body and throw the pieces into Lake Ontario. If they were found later, everyone would think that a soldier had been the victim of hostile Indians.

He began his grisly work. Using his already bloodied sword, he first cut off the head and ran with it to the lake. Returning, he noticed the blood he had left on the floor and, finding some rags, mopped it up quickly. Ready to resume his horrible task, he heard the sound of voices from above and realized that the party was ending. The officers and girls would be coming down the stairs at any moment. There was only one thing to do. With all his strength, Jean-Claude carried the body to the well and threw it in. From the depths of the well came a distant splash, and it was done.

The partygoers stumbled back to their barracks in a much more drunken condition than the one in which they had arrived. If there were any who wondered about Henri and Jean-Claude, they probably thought both men had retired to their own quarters. Within the week some of the officers noticed the absence of Henri, and a search was organized, but it was fruitless. There were those, including Onita, who were convinced that Henri had been murdered by Jean-Claude, but they lacked the evidence with which to step forward and accuse him.

Onita was certain that Henri was dead, for she knew he would have come back to her if he had been alive. Several months passed, and she did not have the heart to go to any parties at the Castle. But one September night when there was to be a party, she decided to go, for the purpose of listening and learning whatever she could that might give some clue to Henri's fate.

The girls and officers left the village together, and some were surprised to see Onita, for she had not been to the Castle since the duel. That night she made it a point to mingle with as many of the officers as possible but not to become deeply involved in conversation with any one of them. Her objective was to find someone who was a friend of Henri's and who had been there the night he disappeared. The evening passed, but she was not successful. Finally, as she was preparing to leave with the other girls, a young man named Jacques came up and spoke to her admiringly.

"I know you. You were with Henri the night of the duel. I often admired you, but Henri was my dear friend, and I knew how much he cared about you. Your name was on his lips often."

"Thank you. Perhaps I shall see you again here at the Castle."

Jacques nodded, his face flushed with pleasure.

Two weeks later Jacques went to the Seneca village. It was on a night when the moon was huge and round with a cast to it, sometimes described as "blood on the moon." However often we see it, there is always something ominous about a full moon that is red. Jacques and Onita sat talking with some of the other members of the tribe, and this time it was Onita who brought the subject around to Henri.

But Jacques stopped her. "Onita, it is not wise for us to say too much about it here. Let's go to the Castle."

The building was empty, for it was by now almost midnight, and the men were in the barracks. They sat down on the bottom step of the same stairs where the duel had occurred, and Jacques began to tell her how he had lingered after the others had left on the night of the duel.

"I don't know what I expected. Perhaps that Henri would come back, but he did not. I sat right where we are now."

"And what happened?"

"I thought I heard a noise coming from the well."

"What did you do?"

"I ran. That's what I did."

Onita looked at him accusingly. "And later you began to think that Jean-Claude might have killed him and put his body in the well. Is that right?"

"Yes. I thought of that and also that he might not have been dead. Perhaps I could have saved his life."

They both fell silent. It was almost midnight, time to take Onita back to the village, thought Jacques.

"Hush! Do you hear something?" Onita whispered.

"Yes. Like something scraping against stone?"

"Do you know where it is coming from?"

"My God! Do you mean the well?"

"Yes."

The clock struck midnight.

And then, as the pair watched horror-stricken, the fingers of a blood-stained hand crept very slowly over the side of the well. A second hand scrabbled over the rim. Now the forearms of a man emerged, dressed in a soldier's uniform. The arms appeared to pull mightily, and as they did, the shoulders and upper portion of a man's body rose out of the well. Where the neck and head should have been, though, there was nothing at all, only a bloody stump.

Jacques and Onita fled, terrified. There was no doubt in their minds that Jean-Claude had murdered Henri and dropped his headless body into the well. Nor did Jacques keep what he had seen a secret. The well was explored, the body of the dead man was found, and Jean-Claude was hanged.

But those who have been there when the full moon is high over the Castle say that, exactly at midnight, the ghost of the headless Frenchman begins to claw its way slowly but surely out of the well. After resting from its efforts, the ghost of Henri Le Clerc rises, dripping, and moves slowly and awkwardly through the dark halls of the Castle in search of its long-lost head.

Old Fort Niagara is a State Historic Site opened by the Old Fort Niagara Association, Inc., in cooperation with the New York State Office of Parks, Recreation, and Historic Preservation. The address is Old Fort Niagara, Fort Niagara State Park, Youngstown, New York 14174. Telephone: (716) 745–7611. Tours are conducted throughout the year.

THE GOVERNOR'S HAUNTED MANSION

Woodburn, Dover, Delaware

When Governor Charles L. Terry of Delaware selected as an executive mansion an eighteenth-century Dover house, it appealed to him and his wife as a stately, serene old home. It was also one of the finest examples of Federal architecture in America. Woodburn was built in 1790 by John Hillyard on a tract given to his great-grandfather by William Penn. The brick is a soft, mellow mauve; the windows are large, and the fanlight over the front door sparkles in the sunlight. It is surrounded by tall pines and trim English boxwoods.

Governor Terry did not concern himself with stories that the house was haunted. But there is at least one person who will forever believe in the apparitions of Woodburn and in the ghost stories—especially the one about the hanging of a slave-catcher. In his seventies now, Albert Pennington Cooper is one of the craftsmen who have done restorative work on the 205-year-old mansion.

One October afternoon, when he and his helper, Troy, were almost ready to leave, a storm came up suddenly.

Here is how Cooper tells the story.

One moment we had plenty of light, but within the half hour it was as dark outside as if it were night. The wind was blowing so fiercely and the branches waving so violently, I thought some of those big trees were going to go. Then rain came down so hard and so heavy that for a while, it was pelting the house like buckshot.

We didn't know whether a tornado was going by or just a bad storm. We would have been drenched if we had tried to make a run for the trucks. So Troy and I sat down inside to wait for it to pass over. The next thing we knew, there was the sound of voices. Strong vibrations shook the whole house. You might have thought that it was from the storm, but when Troy and I looked at each other, I knew he didn't think the racket was wind or rain. Neither did I. It was like an angry undertone of voices, and above it I heard a shriller sound, more like a woman screaming than a man shouting.

"Troy, I'm going to find out what's in that basement," I said. I started down the stairs with my flashlight aimed ahead of me. The noise grew louder. Right behind me came Troy, with a hammer in his hand. Whatever was down there, he was ready for it. At that moment the voices suddenly became quieter, and we began to hear the sound of hurrying footsteps from below.

When we reached the basement, it was brighter than I had expected. In fact, I dropped the flashlight to my side, for we didn't need the light. What could be illuminating the basement so I don't know. Strange figures moved in the room. Have you ever seen cloud forms that resemble people? We all have, but not like these.

I wondered if Troy saw them, too. "What do you see, Troy?" I whispered, and I don't know why I whispered except that all around me, everything was now dead silence. The forms were shifting expressively, and at the same time, they were becoming more distinct. They were taking on the substance and shape of men and women!

"I see some people over at the end of the basement, and the way they move, they're scared, Al," he replied. I saw them, too, but I wanted to hear what he thought. He said, "They're all huddled up together, and I think some are crying."

There was a rattling noise and the sound of something dragging along the floor.

"Chains! Hear them?" asked Troy. Now the smoky figures seemed to mill about, pushing and shoving as if in a panic. Then came a loud crash that actually hurt our ears. It was real; you couldn't doubt that. It struck me as being like the noise of iron bars falling to the ground. On and on it went, the metallic ring traveling through the house, one clanking echo after another.

Troy and I took those basement stairs two at a time and slammed the door behind us. It didn't matter what kind of storm was going on, we were ready to leave. We gathered up our tools and were outside before you could say Jackie Robinson! And you know, the storm had stopped, and the sun was setting in a clear sky.

"That last crash was enough to wake the dead wasn't it, Troy?" I asked.

He took me by the arm, and those big eyes of his wore the strangest look I'd ever seen in them as he said, "Al, what do you mean, wake the dead? Those were the dead."

Well, that really gave me the creeps. Every Sunday, regular as clockwork, my wife and I are at St. Paul's Methodist, and the Bible verse that came to my mind suddenly was "If a man die, shall he live again?"

I asked Troy, "Were they dead or alive?"

"Man, I don't know. We can't go where they are, 'cause that's a notch up the ladder. But they sure can get back here." And with that he drove off in his old battered blue pickup. Now, Troy was just a helper. He didn't have a bunch of degrees and such, but I always envied him for what he did have: a special way of talking to the Lord and getting answers.

That was on a Friday, and I wouldn't need Troy there at the house again until I was finished with some of my own work. That would probably be a couple of weeks, so Monday I was back alone.

Woodburn, the Delaware Governor's House, is home to three ghosts.

I spent the entire morning listening to every sound, just waiting for something to happen. But all that week Woodburn was just as peaceful and quiet as you please, and I was beginning to think that the storm had given me a super case of the jitters.

The second week it seemed to me the house was extra quiet. Sometimes in these places a hundred or more years old, you get used to creaks and the sound of the wind exploring the crevices. After a week or two, it's as if the house is talking under its breath. Maybe it's talking to itself or to the folks who once lived there, but not to you. So you don't pay it any mind.

On Thursday night I had to go out and have myself a little fun, and I stayed up way too late. I was on the job at Woodburn by seven-thirty the next morning, and by midafternoon I was dragging. There was one more task that I needed to do in the house that day, but it would take close attention to do it just right. Since I had priced the work at Woodburn by the job, if I wanted to take a thirty- or forty-minute nap, it was nobody's business but mine. I folded up a jacket for a pillow, pulled my coat up over me, and was soon fast asleep.

At three-thirty I was awakened by a tremendous crash, a noise that rolled and reverberated through the house, apparently coming from the lower level. I got up and looked out the window. It was a gray day, but with no storm in sight. Then a terrible series of rattling and banging began that shook the entire room. I could tell all of this was coming from inside the house. If it had been anywhere but Dover, I would have thought I was in an earthquake.

It reminded me of the afternoon when Troy had been here during the storm, so I made up my mind to go to the basement. I had no sooner gotten down there than I was aware of smoke, but there was no fire to be seen, and the smoke didn't smell like burning wood or oily rags.

For the first minute or so, I couldn't see a thing, but when I did, there were the figures like Troy and I had seen before. Only this time, three were much clearer than the rest. They were a woman and two men. I saw one of the men lift up his hand and drop what seemed to be a large, fat coil of smoke down over the other's head. When he did, there were the most terrible sounds I ever heard, for the man's screams merged with eerie cries of glee from the crowd of figures. A loud, thunderous crash sounded again, and there were such strong vibrations, they went right through me. I don't know what happened after that.

When I came to, I was lying on the floor in the upstairs hall, a few feet from the basement door. I got up and went into the big living room, and there was some light coming in the big windows and making a path across the floor. It was night by now, and there was a moon.

There was also something else—and it was in the house with me. I walked cautiously into the hall. It was coming up from the basement; there was a muffled, clanking sound on each step. I heard it stop in front of the door to the stairs, but the door never opened. Instead, I saw a dark shadow on the door, and the outline of a man's figure began to emerge. Gradually, it came right through that door, and there, a few feet from me, stood the apparition.

I gasped and stepped back, but he never once looked my way. He was not so distinct that I could tell anything about the color of his clothes, but he was clear enough for me to know him for a man.

I thought of the stories about Woodburn, stories of a secret tunnel that connects this house with the St. Jones River behind it, stories of when Woodburn belonged to a Quaker named Daniel Cowgill and was a busy stop on the Underground Railway. In the years before the Civil War, runaway slaves from Maryland and all over the South were sheltered here until Cowgill could help them on their way to Canada or a free state. Sometimes the slave-catchers would raid the house and take runaways back by force.

I'm ashamed now that I didn't take off after that strange figure as I watched him head toward the front door, but I didn't. I sat down on the floor with my back to the wall, and my hand shook so, it took me three tries to light up a cigarette and calm down some.

I didn't want to follow any ghost or even get out to my van, for, if I did, I would have to walk right past its destination. If the specter was the slave-catcher who had met his end here, I was sure he was headed straight for the hanging tree. There was no way I wanted to see a body hanging from that gnarled, old tulip poplar out there in the yard, the tree with the hook embedded in its hollow.

Either I passed out again or I went to sleep briefly, but when I next looked out the window, the moon was high in the sky. I had to get out of there. As I hurried out toward my van, gusts of wind like strong fingers flung wet leaves through the air and sometimes in my face. I didn't turn my head. Then I recalled my tools. Should I leave them until next morning or go back to the house and get them? I turned around, and, when I did, my eyes were inevitably drawn toward the big poplar and to the hollow in its trunk.

There it was! The sight I had dreaded to see: In the moonlight hung the struggling body of a man, twisting and turning, this way and that, suspended by a rope from the hook in the old hanging tree. I turned and ran. On the way home in the van it was hard for me to think, I was so frightened.

Why should I hear and see all that? My great-grandfather Pennington was a slave in Maryland who ran away from his master. He went through Delaware on his way north—maybe even through Dover.

But what did that have to do with me? Had I seen my own great-grandfather here in the basement and not known it? Was he one of those ghost figures who had hanged the slave-catcher?

This is one of several ghost stories in connection with Woodburn, located at 151 King's Highway, Dover, Delaware. In the house also reside a colonial gentleman, a ghost who is a wine bibber, and a little girl in a red-and-white-checked gingham dress. For tour information, call (302) 736-5656.

THE PHANTOM LADY

Mordecai House and the Andrew Johnson Home, Raleigh, North Carolina

Surely a city that has no ghosts is a dull place. Was Raleigh, North Carolina, such a city? It seemed, for a while, that it might be. No one at the Cameron Village Branch of the Raleigh Library knew of any ghosts in the capital city. Its files held no clippings of recent newspaper stories reporting a local apparition. From the standpoint of ghostly presences, everything was all right in Fayetteville, Asheville, Wilmington, and even Charlotte. But not in Raleigh.

Raleigh had politics but no ghosts . . . unless you counted the bed in the Governor's Mansion, from which a mysterious rapping sound was once rumored to emanate. As this occurred while a Democrat was in office, however, Republicans were not inclined to regard it too seriously.

Nor are ghostly presences enough; you also need a haunted house. North Carolina was understandably miffed by being one of the few states not included in a United States Tourist Bureau list of those with haunted houses. On one side was South Carolina, with Alice of the Hermitage; to the west was Tennessee, with the Bell Witch; and most humiliating of all, on its northern border was Virginia, with an entire register of haunted houses!

Such a situation could make a proud state, full of colorful history and mountain scenery, seem almost prosaic. Of course, it

President Andrew Johnson's birthplace, where lighted candles have been seen in the windows

had a beautiful ghost hitchhiker, the famed Brown Mountain Lights, and Joe Baldwin's ghost at Maco. There was surprisingly little else, though, that was noteworthy.

But now new specters have come to the rescue.

Not far from the heart of Raleigh is a small historic park called Mordecai Square. Its most impressive building is the large Mordecai Manor itself, with its many wings. Also on the square is a quaint building once used as a law office; a village chapel; a tiny house in which our seventeenth president, Andrew Johnson, was born; and a small, early building used for an office by the Raleigh Historic Properties Commission.

On the afternoon that I called Historic Properties, good fortune was heaped up and spilling over. Terry Myers was there, and I asked her my question: Did she know of any ghost stories in connection with any of the historic properties? Indeed, she did! But not so fast. What sort of person was Ms. Myers? Was she reliable? It was reassuring to learn that she was a knowledgeable, charming lady full of enthusiasm about North Carolina history. A former schoolteacher from Arizona who inspired her students to do special history and folklore projects, she had moved to Raleigh and begun working for Historic Properties. This next ghost-story account is her own experience.

"One November afternoon I wanted to complete a project at work, and, without noticing it, I worked on well after everyone else had left. When I realized that it was time to leave, it was dark outside, but I've never been afraid here."

Outside, the lanterns on the tall posts along the street cast their warm, yellow light on the buildings and gave the restoration life. One could imagine women in these houses engaged in meal preparation, and the lawyers had doubtless just left their offices and were somewhere sipping a glass of sherry before supper. Just as autumn is a time between summer and winter to pause and reflect, so, too, dusk is a time of day to pause and ruminate by the hearthside upon the day's events.

Inside the Historic Properties office, Terry put the papers she had been working on to rest. Arising from her desk somewhat stiffly, for she had been sitting there for a long time, she slipped into her dark blue coat and was ready to leave. Standing on the porch outside, she could smell the woodsmoke from someone's fireplace, and then her sensible, low-heeled navy pumps were crunching along on fallen leaves, noisy as tissue wrappings. The sound was a satisfying one, nature shedding its garment from the previous season.

Terry approached the lamppost in front of the tiny, gambrel-roofed house in which President Andrew Johnson was born in 1808. This early-nineteenth-century environment had become so real to her that sometimes modern streetlights could be jarring. She had left late like this before, but tonight, at the edges of her mind, she was aware that something was different.

What could it be?

Then Terry became aware of a light. Had a lamp been left on that should have been turned off in one of the buildings, or was there a glow through the crack of a door that should not have been left ajar? Were a car's parking lights reflecting in a window?

She felt uneasy. Was someone else here on the square tonight, and was that person carrying a flashlight or a lantern? This thought caused her to stop, for if that were the case, she would stand back beside the office building in the darkness until the person passed. Whoever it was would likely walk along from the direction of Mordecai House, past the stone marker in front of the Andrew Johnson Birthplace, and head toward the street.

She heard the furtive rustle of leaves and shrank back against the building. The sound grew closer, and she could feel the thump of her heart. Then there was a sudden flurry in the leaves just a few

Who was the phantom lady seen recently in the historic Mordecai House at Raleigh, North Carolina? Will she reappear?

feet from her, and she almost ran. Instead, she stayed perfectly still. More rustling. Perhaps whoever it was had seen her and knew that in a moment she would be flushed out like a frightened bird from its hiding place.

Suddenly, something white darted from the blackness past her. She almost fainted until she saw with relief that it was only a large cat, probably chasing its prey. She stepped back on the path, and it was then, for the first time, that she looked squarely at the single downstairs window in the tiny house that was the birthplace of the seventeenth president. In that window was the source of her uneasiness.

Suspended there, as if held in the center of the small window by an invisible human hand, was a candle, its bright flame silhouetted against the blackness of the room within. It seemed to hang there interminably. Terry stood staring at it. There was no reason for anyone to be inside that house with a candle. Then, with the flame appearing ready to go out at any moment, the candle began to move away from the window, and within seconds it was gone. But not for long—a moment later it reappeared, this time in the second-story window.

Terry was genuinely frightened. Someone or something was in that house. She turned and ran toward the safety of the street. When she had reached it, she looked back, just in time to see the candle, until then burning steadily in the tiny upstairs window, go out as suddenly as if extinguished by a hand.

Was it a ghost? If so, Terry had seen enough.

"That is the only time anything has happened to me that was eerie or out of the ordinary. I was later told that realtors had seen the same thing.

"By the way," continued Terry, "Rosa Burt has an unusual story, if she will tell it. Rosa is the housekeeper at the Mordecai House."

Mordecai House dominates the square. It was built in 1785 by a planter named Joel Lane, but it acquired its name and fame from one of the first Jews to settle in Raleigh. A gentleman of education and means, Moses Mordecai married the Lanes' daughter, Ellen.

Mordecai and his bride retained William Nichols, a noted Southern architect, to remodel the house. Behind a Greek Revival double portico is a double-doored entrance hall and five large rooms. It was the earliest example of this type of architecture to be built in Raleigh.

Most historic homes are furnished with pieces donated or purchased that are compatible with the period of the house, but the furnishings here were actually the belongings of its early families. They lived daily with these portraits, pictures, books, and furniture.

Perhaps their attachment to some of these things may be the key to Rosa Burt's unusual experience.

Rosa is not a superstitious person, but she will never understand an experience that she had one morning at Mordecai House. There is a long hallway down the center of the house, and at the end of it is the library. On the right of the hall is the parlor; on the left, the dining room. She remembers exactly what happened.

"I was there one afternoon, cleaning when the house was closed to visitors, and I was just finishing up in the dining room. There I stood in the doorway, wiping down the woodwork, when I saw what I supposed to be one of the docents [guides] walking up the hall toward me from the library. The lady wore a long, black pleated skirt and a white middy-type blouse with a black tie.

"I stood and watched, puzzled, because they don't usually come on days when I am cleaning. She didn't even look over at me as she came down the hall. I remember thinking that she might at least nod her head or act like I existed, but she didn't. She came walking along just like she owned the place, head in the air and looking straight ahead. Then, when she was right opposite me, she turned and went through the parlor doorway across the hall.

"While I was out in the hall working, I think I was expecting her to make some noise or come out. But all was quiet, and she did not reappear. Finally, I decided to see what was going on. I walked over to the parlor door and looked in. When I did, there wasn't a soul in there. That room was empty as it could be. This gave me a real start, for I knew I had seen her go in, and, if she had come out, she would have had to pass by me. There wasn't any other way out.

"You can imagine how this stayed on my mind. I knew all of the women who were guides, and she certainly was not one of them. But even though she wasn't one of the guides, I knew her face was familiar.

"Finally, I thought, why, she looks just like Margaret Lane. She was a pretty thing, and I'd seen her picture many a time when I was cleaning." Margaret Lane was an early resident of the house.

"Sometimes, even now, I find myself going over and over it in my mind, thinking, how did it happen?"

Rosa looked down the hall in the direction of the library. "All I know is that she went into that room and never came out of it. Mmm. If I saw that sort of thing often, my nerves wouldn't take it!"

Rosa still wonders: Will she ever again see the apparition of the woman who lived here more than two centuries ago?

The Mordecai House and the Andrew Johnson Home are at 1 Mimosa Street, Raleigh, North Carolina. They are open to the public. Admission is free, but hours vary. More information may be obtained by calling (919) 834–4844.

THE FREE SPIRIT

Ashton Villa, Galveston, Texas

James Brown of Galveston was a proud man. He was proud of the fortune he had made in the hardware business, of building the first brick house in the state, of being a Texan, and of his daughter Bettie.

But as time went on, it appeared that Bettie had a tragic flaw.

Her home was the palatial Ashton Villa—fortunately completed in 1859, for, due to the Civil War, nothing was built from 1861 to 1865. Galveston was blockaded during the greater part of the war, first captured by the Federals in October of 1862 and then recaptured three months later by the Confederates.

Born in 1855, "Miss Bettie," a lovely, golden-haired child, lived in an exciting atmosphere. During the war years the house served as a hospital for Confederate soldiers, and, as Galveston was alternately in the hands of both armies, serving as a headquarters for both, Union and Confederate generals came and went. Over and over again it has been said in Galveston that the swords of surrender were exchanged between the North and South in the Gold Room, Ashton Villa's ornate, formal living room.

Soon after the war ended, Galveston began to regain its prosperity. Wharves were again crowded with ships laden with merchandise, old stores were remodeled, and new ones were opened. Wartime damage was repaired, and returning soldiers came home to resume their trades and professions. It was a bustling port. The late 1800s arrived, and with them Galveston became a celebrated trading center. Ships from around the world dropped anchor in its busy harbor. Fortunes were made overnight, and The Strand, the business district of this seaside city, became "the Wall Street of the Southwest."

One of the most picturesque and romantic cities in the South, it was the perfect setting for a beautiful woman. Here Rebecca Ashton Brown, the favorite daughter of financier James M. Brown, lived an adventurous life, the likes of which most Victorian ladies did not dare even imagine. A legend in her own time, she scandalized many with her liberated ways. She often traveled alone, smoked in public, and never married—shocking for a woman of her day.

Miss Bettie, as she was most often known, was the epitome of the frivolity and opulence that the period exuded. A free spirit, she traveled to Munich, Dusseldorf, and other art centers of Europe. Preferring travel and adventure to giving up her freedom, Miss Bettie rejected marriage but had many beaux. One of them even quaffed champagne from her gilded slipper.

Nine years after the end of the Civil War, a fashionable summer resort for the wealthy opened in Waukesha, Wisconsin. It was called Fountain Spring House, and the arrival at its doors of a Southern belle from Galveston, Texas, was reported in the *Milwaukee Journal.* "She made her appearance with sixteen trunks filled with such finery as Waukesha never before beheld on one woman; and with her carriage, her liverymen, servants, a coachman, and coal-black horses." The other guests at the hotel were stunned by such a display.

Her beauty was emphasized by her magnificent gowns, and it was said that Miss Bettie often appeared in three different costumes in one day. It was always she who led the grand marches. At one Christmas ball she wore a handsome, black-velvet princess gown.

Miss Bettie was a free spirit—so free that there are some who believe that even after death she was able to return to beautiful Ashton Villa.

On its train were leaves embossed in solid gold, and in her hand she carried an enormous ostrich fan studded with real pearls. That night her golden-haired Grecian beauty was a striking contrast to the appearance of her escort, an arrestingly handsome man with black hair and a beard. This was one of the few nights when Miss Bettie seemed to laugh delightedly and talk attentively to her escort. In repose, her face had come to look more and more unhappy.

Her frequent trips abroad were an occasion to collect art objects and curios, paintings, and tapestries from many foreign lands. Among her favorites were costumes and a collection of unusual fans. These treasures were kept in a small alcove in Ashton Villa's ornate living room, called the Gold Room, where she often entertained.

In 1920 she died, still a mysterious and enigmatic woman. The mansion once so full of life, became a museum. The house was beautifully restored with Miss Bettie's paintings and her furniture. The Gold Room is as beautiful a showplace today as it was when she was alive.

The villa's carriage house has often been used as living quarters for a caretaker. This is where Terry O'Donohoe stayed one weekend to fill in for a friend named Don Ross, the tall, darkly handsome young man who was then caretaker of the mansion. Illness in the family necessitated Ross's being away overnight. Nothing was said to anyone: O'Donohoe simply took Ross's place. It is doubtful that anyone even knew O'Donohoe was not the regular caretaker.

Just before O'Donohoe went to bed that night, he noticed some heat lightning and the oppressive stillness of the air outside. "We're going to get some rain," he thought. Buffy, Ross's dog, was behaving peculiarly, following him everywhere and underfoot constantly. What was wrong with the animal? Perhaps Ross was used to this, but it was getting on O'Donohoe's nerves. He decided to put the dog outside.

Sometime after midnight he was awakened by an ear-shattering crash of thunder, followed by smaller volleys close by. The dog was barking wildly. O'Donohoe's first thought was that someone was trying to break into the mansion, and, mindful of his duty, he hurriedly threw on his clothes. Outdoors the rain lashed at him angrily, and one bolt of lightning after another erupted over his head. It was a devil of a night. He dashed under the canopy of huddled trees near the villa, but nothing was any protection against the storm, and he was drenched.

Inside the villa, O'Donohoe's first impression was that the house could not have been any quieter. He had turned on the lights and already checked two rooms, however, when he heard people talking. It was a man and a woman, their voices raised in angry argument. Shrinking back against the wall, O'Donohoe had almost convinced himself that someone with a right to be in the house had come back unexpectedly when he realized that all was again quiet.

O'Donohoe waited for about five minutes, then he decided to continue his check of the house. When he reached the Gold Room, he was certain that he heard a rustling sound coming from within the room, but what could it be? His fingers found the light switch just inside the door, and for a moment the room was ablaze with light. To his astonishment, he saw a woman seated at the piano and a man looking down at her. He flipped the switch off instantly.

He was sure that the pair had seen him, and at any moment he expected them to come after him. How could he explain who he was and what he was doing there at one o'clock in the morning? They would summon the police. He quickly stepped behind a screen. On the other hand, what were *they* doing there in the darkness? But even as he wondered, he had a strange feeling, a feeling that somehow they belonged there and he did not.

Moonlight was streaming in the windows, and his eyes soon adjusted to it. He watched the woman. What a beauty she was, with that golden hair piled on top of her head. She put a handkerchief up to her eyes and seemed to be crying. The man, tall with dark, curly hair and a beard, was talking to her. Suddenly, it was as if a dial had been turned up on a radio, for he could hear their conversation as clearly as if they were right beside him.

"Bettie, do you know who Narcissus fell in love with when he looked in the pool?"

"He fell in love with his own beauty. But what are you trying to say?"

"It is foolish for any man to talk to you about marriage. You are like Narcissus. You are unable to love anyone. You are completely absorbed in your own pleasure, collecting meaningless objects, and, most of all, your looks."

"Harrison, do you really believe the cruel things you are saying about me?"

"I've come to know you too well, Bettie."

"I won't listen to this. You are hateful!" And with her chin stubbornly tilted upward and eyes straight ahead, she began playing the piano.

The man paced back and forth for a few minutes with an angry look on his face. And then he was gone. There was a crashing chord as the woman struck the keys violently. She dropped her head on her arms on the piano, and O'Donohoe heard her sobbing.

He was about to leave as quietly as possible when the lady wiped her eyes, arose from the piano bench, and looked in his direction. For a moment he almost panicked and ran, for he thought a sound had betrayed him. She walked over toward some shelves filled with art objects. What an unusual dress she was wearing, O'Donohoe thought, but how it became her. It must be a costume out of the 1800s. Now she was not far from where he was concealed behind a Chinese screen. Standing in front of the shelves, with her back to him, she reached up with her right hand and, taking something off the shelf, held it in front of her. What in heaven's name was she looking at? She turned around, and once more he was struck by her beauty.

She held an exquisite fan in her hands.

"Mirror, mirror on the wall. Who is the fairest one of all . . ." she began to recite in low, melodic tones. With the fan beside her own lovely face, she stared into the mirror.

The fan fell from her hand. Even as O'Donohoe gazed, fascinated, her lovely face seemed to fade, and then to disappear.

By morning the experience seemed more like a dream to

O'Donohoe. The regular caretaker, Ross, returned early and stopped by the villa for a few minutes. When he eventually came to the carriage house, he was filled with excitement.

"Terry, you won't be able to believe it, but early this morning a valuable fan was taken from Miss Bettie's collection, and it was found on the floor. Can you imagine that?"

"No."

"Someone must have a strange sense of humor."

"I suppose so."

"The cleaning lady found it when she was vacuuming this morning. Didn't you hear her call?"

"No. I didn't hear a thing."

"Terry, why do you have such a strange expression on your face? You look as if you aren't telling me everything. If something happened last night over at the villa, you need to say so, because I'm responsible."

"Responsible?"

"Yes, responsible. I'm responsible for Miss Bettie's house. Now tell me what happened."

Terry told him how he had woken up when he heard the storm and the dog barking, how he thought someone was breaking into the mansion, and how, still not sure but that it might be burglars, he had cautiously entered the house and seen the couple in the Gold Room. When he got to the part about Miss Bettie carrying the fan over to the mirror, his voice began to tremble. Ross was greatly excited.

"What did you think of her? Isn't she gorgeous? How did she look when you saw her last night?"

"Golden hair on top of her head, tall, great figure."

"She's a real beauty, all right. There's not a woman alive who can match Miss Bettie."

"Don, there isn't any way I would check on that house again at night. It's haunted, and by more than one ghost. There was a man, dark, handsome . . ."

Ross interrupted in some agitation. "And did she seem to care for him?"

"Great heavens, man. How should I know? We're talking about a ghost, don't you understand?"

But Don Ross didn't really seem to be listening. He was examining his face intently in the mirror. Then he searched the dark, curly hair and beard for gray. "How strange he is," thought O'Donohoe, as he watched him. He had just met Ross a few weeks ago. Maybe after he had known him longer . . . but O'Donohoe wasn't really sure he wanted to.

"I don't think we need to mention anything about your experience in the villa." Ross patted him on the shoulder. "It will be our secret," he said as O'Donohoe left.

Ross looked at his watch. One o'clock in the afternoon, and he was already eager for the time to pass. He knew that if the dog barked, he would go. Suppose she *was* only a vision. She was the most beautiful, romantic-looking woman he had ever seen. He would never leave her.

Ashton Villa and nearby historic buildings attract tourists the year around. For information, write Ashton Villa, Galveston Historical Foundation, 2328 Broadway, Galveston, Texas 77550. Historic preservation and the lure of the Gulf Coast have made Galveston as glamorous a place today as it was in the late 1800s, when Miss Bettie lived in the villa.

THE DREADED MEETING

White Oaks, Charlotte, North Carolina

It is hard to live for a quarter of a century in a city the size of Charlotte, North Carolina, and not hear some fascinating ghost stories. But when that city is home, you know its family connections, and you are aware that others do, too. Will they recognize someone or even themselves, and how much embarrassment will a story cause?

Keeping to the facts, but with some disguising of names, we will take that risk and relate a story for those interested in the supernatural. Since I was a confidante of the woman in this story, I was able to keep up with the events. She was a writer, and her occupation caused her to meet many well-to-do Charlotteans—but it would be far better if I were to let the young woman, whom we will call Karen, tell the experience in her own words.

I had an assignment to do a story on an historic house called White Oaks. My interview was set for late in the afternoon, and the hostess had told me that there would be a party going on for a performing-arts group.

"Your presence won't be any inconvenience at all, Karen. In fact, why not plan to just be one of my guests and enjoy yourself," she suggested graciously.

When a story subject had to cancel, I decided to go home early and change from a tailored suit into a new red cocktail dress that was infinitely more flattering. I remember thinking how foolish it was, but something overruled my usual practicality, and as I drove down Providence Road in all my finery, I was excited about the evening ahead.

When I first saw the colonial mansion, I thought that Scarlett O'Hara would certainly have felt at home here. Once owned by the late James Buchanan Duke, this stately sixty-five-year-old house in the heart of Charlotte's Eastover section stands almost as tall as the branches of the towering trees that surround it. White Oaks, as it is called, was part of that grand scale of living to which Duke, a tobacco king, was accustomed.

I knocked, thinking the butler would answer. The door opened almost immediately, and there stood not the butler, but the most handsome man I had ever seen. He had dark, curly hair with a distinguished hint of gray, expressive blue-green eyes, and a dazzling smile. In a charming and amusing fashion, he pretended to be the butler. We were both laughing as we walked together down the white-and-black-marble entrance hall. He introduced me to a group of other guests, who stood chatting and sampling hors d'oeuvres at one end of an elegant room the size of a ballroom.

My impromptu escort was obviously the center of the women's attention, and he had no sooner introduced himself to me as Jon than two plump ladies came up and, with an arm through each of his, carried him off. He appeared to be drifting away on a pair of water wings and looked back as if reluctant to go.

"Oh, here you are," said my hostess, appearing at my elbow. "Everyone seems to be entertaining themselves. This is a good time to take you on a tour of the house. It has changed considerably since Nanaline Duke lived here, but I doubt if she would mind the changes we've made."

"Oh, did the Dukes live here long?" I asked.

"Only for about six years, and Nanaline far less than her hus-

White Oaks, a historic Charlotte house where a promise resulted in a startling, macabre experience.

band or daughter. She made no bones about finding Charlotte dull, and when they visited here, she usually left before the rest of her family."

I gazed admiringly at the hand-carved marble fireplace at one end of the room. The gold leaf in this room was lovely. "That was applied by the Dukes. We used masking tape to protect it while we were repainting," my hostess commented. A round oak table looked almost lost in the oversize kitchen, and along one side wall was an immense, hooded gas range that had been used by the servants of former families.

There were beautiful classical mantles, marble hearths, and tiles around the fireplaces. Bathroom fixtures were early ceramic castings, and there were elaborately detailed brass fixtures. Some of the lighting resembled Colonial candles or oil lamps. In the dining room was one of the most magnificent crystal chandeliers I had ever seen.

My hostess suddenly turned and asked, "Have you and Jon Avery known each other long?"

"I met him tonight. Why do you ask?"

"It's just that he is married. His wife has been in a sanatorium for the last three years."

"I'm sorry to hear that, but, really, that is the first conversation I have ever had with him, and probably the last." As if to make me out a liar, there was a masculine voice at my elbow, and it was Jon's.

"I've brought you some champagne, caviar, and a sandwich. I hope this will lure you into talking with me, Karen."

"How can I resist such thoughtfulness?" I asked, genuinely hungry. What possible harm could there be in spending a few minutes with this man?

For the first time I noticed that he had a slight limp. Someone nearby was talking about track, I believe. At any rate, we both heard the conversation, and he turned to me, saying, "I'm sure you've noticed my limp. It's the result of polio when I was a child. I used to resent the fact that I came along before Dr. Salk and his sugar cubes with vaccine in them."

"You met me at the door and escorted me in, and I certainly wasn't aware of it then," I said, which was true.

This seemed to please him greatly, and he went on to tell me that, through hours of exercise, he had become able to play volleyball in college and since then had walked at least three miles a day. We went on to talk of current events and his hobby of photography.

Thinking it over later, I could not deny that I found this man attractive. He had a charming smile. I had enjoyed our talk very much, but figured that was where it ended.

The next day was Friday, and I picked up the phone at my office to hear Jon Avery's voice asking if I would join him for dinner. I had plans for the evening with a new executive who had come to the paper from another city. We had lunched together several times, and it was just a friendship. I could have changed our dinner to another night, but I could not forget my hostess's warning. I was polite, but my voice held Jon at arm's length as I told him I had other plans. That should be it.

Less than a week had passed when I was surprised by a call from White Oaks with an invitation to return. My hostess was having a few people over for drinks, and among them were a couple who had once lived in the house. If I had not finished my story, she wondered, would I care to talk to them? Of course, I accepted.

We had been seated on the brick terrace at White Oaks for less than an hour when the doorbell rang. In a few minutes I heard the faint sound on the terrace of someone walking with a limp. For some insane reason, I could feel my heart thud. Of course, it was Jon, and I felt that he was as surprised to see me as I was to see him.

How beautiful it was that afternoon, with the blooms of dogwoods, cherry trees, and azaleas. The other guests went off to tour the house, and Jon suggested that I might like to go out and look at the gardens and fountains. "Buck" Duke had done everything well, and there was nothing like it anywhere else in Charlotte. How long we stood talking at the edge of a circular garden near the fountains, I have no idea. But I know that when we rejoined the others and my hostess looked at me, I felt some guilt and embarrassment.

Something had happened that evening between Jon and me, and during the coming months, it seemed to block my fear of consequences and normal feelings of guilt. When I did consider the future, it was with all sorts of romantic imaginings. His wife would probably not live long, and he was aware of it; or he would divorce her, and we would move to another city after setting up a generous trust for her lifetime care. All obstacles would somehow miraculously disappear, melted by the fervency of our love for each other.

But in August I began to realize that Jon's sense of responsibility would never allow him to divorce his wife, and anything other than marriage would be impossible for me. More and more I began to feel sorry for this woman I had never met.

What was the answer to this painful situation? The only right decision was to end my doomed romance.

One night, as I left Queens Road and turned down Ardsley, I knew I must not weaken. Jon had arrived first. There was a large party going on at White Oaks, and just as we had on that fateful evening in the early spring, we walked again in the gardens. Everything about Jon's manner—the tension, the pleading expression in his eyes—told me he sensed what I planned to tell him.

Afterward, we were both in agony and stood silently together near a fountain. What could be said to assuage such hurt?

"I must go now. I really must." I looked at my watch; it was midnight.

"Karen, do just one thing for me, please. It is all I shall ever ask of you on this earth."

"What is it?"

"I will agree to all you have said. Just promise to meet me here one year from tonight at the same hour."

I was reluctant at first, thinking how difficult it would be to see him and how bad it would be for us both, as it would only reopen partly healed wounds. But at last I consented.

"Well, I'll come if I'm alive." I said, with an attempt at lightness.

Jon grasped me by the wrist. "Don't say that, Karen. Say dead or alive!"

"All right, then. We will meet, dead or alive." Thus we parted.

The next year I was on the same spot a few minutes before the appointed time, and Jon arrived punctually at midnight. I had begun to regret the arrangement I had made, but it was a promise. Although I kept this appointment, I said that I really did not wish to do so again. Jon, however, persuaded me to renew it for just one more year, and I consented, much against my better judgment. We again said our goodbyes, repeating the promise, "Dead or alive."

I had begun to see a delightful man, and late the following spring, we became engaged. The summer was spent boating on Lake Norman, with occasional trips to visit Alex's family in the North Carolina mountains at Montreat. They were prominent Presbyterians, his father active and respected in the denomination. We were planning a September wedding and a honeymoon that would begin on Labor Day weekend.

By early July I had begun to think more and more about my promise to Jon. The last thing I wanted to do was to meet him in the gardens again. The days sped past with terrible swiftness, and the thought of that meeting hung over me like a dark cloud. I didn't want to go, but I had promised. I supposed the only thing that could get me out of it was death. Not even that, really, for I had promised to go dead or alive. Dead or alive! What a macabre promise to ask of me.

I knew very well that Alex wouldn't like me meeting another man in a secluded place at midnight. Should I talk to him with the hope he would understand? Was he likely to understand me once having dated a married man, even one married to an invalid in a sanatorium? Guilt overwhelmed me.

As the last Monday night in July approached, I became more and more apprehensive. If I were to find out about Alex meeting a woman under such peculiar circumstances a short time before our marriage, I would consider calling off the wedding. Would he feel that way if he found out? Finally, I decided I would confide in my long-standing friend and apartment-mate and ask her to accompany me. Sherry said she would go to be sure I was all right.

That night we arrived at the gardens about ten minutes before twelve. I decided I would leave, having kept my promise, if Jon were not there by midnight. The area near the brick terrace was empty, and I did not see a soul. But at five minutes before twelve, I heard a slight noise. It came again. Finally, ever so softly, it was occurring at regular intervals. It was the sound of footsteps on the brick terrace, but they were slower than normal and had just the slightest dragging sibilance. It is he, I thought, for I had heard that walk too often to mistake it. Tonight he was right on time.

I knew that what I must tell him about my approaching marriage would hurt, even though he had surely resigned himself to the end of our romance. The footsteps were coming closer. Soon I would have to break the news about Alex. Sherry was at a discreet distance, but close enough to see me. I stood by the fountain in the brilliant moonlight.

On came the footsteps. Why so slow?

I was not only ashamed to be there but was growing increasingly angry that I had allowed myself to be persuaded to come a second time. This would be our last meeting, and I would not stay long. I could see Jon now, and I watched him make his way into the moonlight at the end of the terrace. On he came, past a large azalea bush and along the drive. It would all be over soon, thank heaven.

When he was close enough for me to see him more clearly, I noticed that he was dressed in dark, formal attire. He must be doing this for its effect, I reasoned, for he knew how handsome I had always thought him in a black coat.

Oddly enough, he seemed about to pass me, and, involuntarily, I reached out my arm with an affectionate gesture to stop him. I was astounded when he walked right through it, and I could feel nothing. As he looked over at me, I distinctly saw his lips move, forming the words, "Dead or alive."

I even heard him say them, not with my ears but with some other sense, what sense I do not know. But the words were spoken as clearly as if they had been said in a normal voice. I felt my blood turn to ice. Hurrying over to where I knew Sherry was standing, I asked "Sherry, who passed you?"

"Let's go. I don't want to talk about it."

"Sherry, you know who I was coming to meet, and he had to pass you. You don't mean you didn't see him."

"I heard him coming. I'd know that walk of his anywhere, and then he went right by only a short distance away. But Karen, there was something wrong, something so strange about him that it scared me to death. Then I saw him stand in front of you. What did he say?" she asked.

"Let's leave. We can talk at home."

And talk we did, for half the night, until finally we went to bed.

The next day I phoned a relative of Jon's on some pretext. I had not spoken to her in months, but almost immediately the conversation turned to Jon.

"You knew he had died, didn't you, Karen?'

"No! I've been out of town."

"It happened last Friday while he was in South Carolina, and we buried him Sunday in the family plot. He had suddenly become ill, and actually was quite delirious toward the end. For the last hour before he died, he kept saying over and over, "Dead or alive! Will I get there?" I wish I could say he had a peaceful death. But poor Jon must have had some terrible fear about reaching the hereafter that none of us ever suspected. How I wish I had known it, so I could have led him to the Lord."

I hung up the phone in a state of shock. Jon had been true to his promise to meet me. He had come even from beyond the grave.

White Oaks, at 400 Hermitage Road, in Charlotte, North Carolina, was built by James Buchanan Duke and is also known as the Duke Mansion. This elegant house is now the Lynnwood Foundation Conference Center. For information please phone (704) 375–4400.

THE PIRATE'S HOUSE
Savannah, Georgia

"You have to take some risk to find adventure," said Marion.

"I don't want adventure, only a decent meal," said her husband. Jack Moore could just taste a good seafood dinner. They had strolled along the Savannah waterfront most of the afternoon, intrigued by the variety of shops housed in the brick buildings that had once been cotton warehouses. At about five-thirty they had begun talking about where to have dinner.

"Let's ask one of the natives," suggested Marion.

Jack groaned. "Do you remember that little hole-in-the-wall in San Diego? The last time you asked a native, it was terrible."

"Look at that man over there, in the faded blue dungarees. I'll bet he would know."

"All right. You ask him, and then I can blame you later."

The man was sitting on a bench, sifting through a number of fishing lures.

"Visitors, are you, and you want to know where to get a good meal? Well, I suppose that depends on your taste and your wallet. Where are you folks from?"

"We're from Massachusetts. Both of our families have always lived on the coast," said Marion.

"Mine, too," he said.

"What do you think of the Pirate's House restaurant?" asked

Jack. "Maybe I ought to indulge my wife. She's always saying that one of her ancestors was a pirate."

"Well, join the club," the man replied. "My grandfather used to say that we were descendants of Captain Bartholomew Roberts, one of the boldest buccaneers of his day. They called him the Crimson Pirate because he often wore red."

"We really ought to introduce ourselves. I'm Marion Moore, and this is my husband, Jack."

"Glad to meet you. I'm Bart Roberts. You were asking about the Pirate's House. The food is fine. I eat there myself now and then, but sometimes some of the goings on there bother me a little." He looked down at the lure he was tying on his line.

"You mean loud music, that sort of thing?"

"No. I didn't mean that."

"Well, then, what bothers you?"

"It's other things. Things like . . . well, it's hard to say."

"Like what?" prodded Marion.

Roberts just looked down at the knot his weathered hands were tying and shook his head. "Don't pay any attention to an old sea dog like myself. You folks will like it. The place has an interesting atmosphere."

"Is your boat tied up near here?"

"That's her right there. The *Mary Anne*. She's named after my wife, although I'm a widower now. I take her out every morning at sunup, and we're back here by late afternoon. Some days the catch is quite good. It certainly beats teaching at a university."

"Where did you teach?" asked Jack.

"The University of Oklahoma."

"And you just left it all?"

"Yep. It gave me the feeling of being landlocked. So I decided to come back home. My family has been in the commercial fishing business here for years."

"Have you ever regretted your decision?"

"No. I have too many seagoing ancestors to want to spend my life in a classroom."

"How about being our guest for dinner?" Jack asked.

"You folks don't need me along."

"It would be a real treat for us. You can tell us about Savannah, and you and Marion can swap pirate stories."

"You've talked me into it. Let me go by my place and change."

"That's great. Marion and I will have a few oysters at a raw bar and then meet you in front of the Pirate's House at seven o'clock."

They were waiting in the parking lot when Bart Roberts drove up. The Pirate's House is a rambling old frame building on East Broad Street, not far from the waterfront, and was once an inn for Savannah seamen. Its shutters are painted blue, a custom along the coast of South Carolina and Georgia. The color blue is believed to be a protection against evil spirits.

"Well, Marion, you and Bart are entering the old haunts of your ancestors," joked Jack as the trio walked up the wooden steps of the porch.

"This part of the city was like the Barbary Coast in Africa," said Bart, after they had ordered. "It was an area where men were drugged and shanghaied; and when they awoke, they found themselves on a vessel out at sea. Not far from this house, the Savannah River forms a half moon, and yet it's still fairly deep. Ships that drew twelve feet of water could ride within ten yards of the bank. My grandfather said that pirates who came here were on the lookout for men and boys to kidnap. They would take them out through an underground passage to the river and load them, unconscious, into a small boat to take them to the ships lying in wait a few yards offshore.

"As time goes, it hasn't been so long since Savannah swarmed with sailors night and day. They were of all nationalities. Many

The Pirate's House in Savannah was once a home for seafaring men such as Flint and Blackbeard. It is now a well-known Savannah restaurant.

were pirates who swaggered along the streets sporting cutlasses, swords, or a brace of pistols. The LaFitte brothers made Savannah their headquarters for a while, and Jean LaFitte married a local girl named Mary Morton."

"Tell me more about the underground passage," said Marion.

"It's here, just as it's always been. But let's eat our meal while it's hot."

They were almost through when Marion said to her husband, "Jack, where are all those loud, rough voices coming from?"

"What in the world are you talking about?"

"It sounds as if some coarse, crude fellow is shouting."

"Do you mean that party at the table over there? They're just having a good time. Don't let it upset you."

"I'm not talking about them." Marion said impatiently. "Jack, don't you hear that man's horrible, loud voice calling out?"

"No, I don't."

Bart laid his hand soothingly on Marion's arm. "I'm not sure I hear what you do, but I do hear an undertone of voices at times."

"Of course, anyone can hear that."

"Marion, tell me what words you hear."

"I'm not sure I can do that, but let's all be quiet for a few minutes, and I'll try." For a little while they were silent, and then Marion's face clouded. "I hear it again."

"What do you hear?"

Her face turned white, and she shook her head. "Bart, do you know where the opening is to the underground tunnel?"

"Yes."

"Jack, do you mind waiting here alone for the check? I want to see that passage."

"Go ahead."

Marion followed Bart out of their dining room into another and still another, until they came to a small storage area.

"It's back here," he said, pushing some furniture to one side. There, in front of them, was a hole in the floor. It was the mouth of a tunnel.

"I don't think we should try to go down there. Do you still hear anything?" asked Bart. Marion shook her head, and he turned to go back.

Suddenly, her hand seized his arm. "Now! That's the voice. Do you hear it?" Bart stepped over to the edge of the tunnel, and his face changed. "Who in the devil . . . that is one of the most evil voices I've ever heard, bar none."

"He's calling me!"

"Tell me what you hear."

"He's calling 'M'Graw' over and over. That was my maiden name! I must go down there!"

"He doesn't mean you," said Bart, grasping Marion's arm. "See if you can make out any other words."

'Darby . . . Darby M'Graw' is what he is saying." By this time they had been joined by Jack.

"What else do you hear?" persisted Bart.

"This is crazy! Let's get her out of here," interrupted Jack, seeing his wife's terrified face.

"Wait a minute, Jack. Now, listen hard and tell me what else you hear, Marion."

She stepped closer to the tunnel. "Just the jumble of voices. No. He's shouting again!"

"And he's saying . . . ?" prompted Bart.

" 'Fetch aft the rum, M'Graw. Fetch me the rum!' That's what he's saying, but why my name?"

"It's not you he's calling. Let's get her out of here, Jack."

"What in Hades was all that about, Bart?"

"Yes, what was it about?" echoed Marion weakly.

"Marion, tell me something," said Bart. "Do you have unusually sensitive hearing? Do noises bother you that don't bother most people?"

"Yes."

"I can't explain what happened back there, but perhaps we can put some of it together." Bart spoke quietly, his voice subdued. "There are many stories about the Pirate's House, but probably the best-authenticated one is that the infamous Captain Flint died there and that his ghost still haunts the rooms of the old building. It's not surprising that his ghost can't rest, for Robert Louis Stevenson wrote that, in sheer wickedness, 'Blackbeard was a child compared to Flint!'

"And Stevenson was right," Bart continued. Some say that Flint was a fictitious pirate, but I think he was real! On the night he died, he was delirious, and he shouted again and again to his shipmate, 'Fetch me some rum.' The name of that shipmate was Darby McGraw!"

"But it seemed to come from the passageway," said Marion, puzzled.

"You heard it when we were sitting at the table, too, didn't you?"

"That's true, I did."

"Have you had experiences like this before, hearing sounds that other people can't?" asked Bart.

"Yes."

"My father was like that, and I share it, but to a much lesser degree. Haven't you seen a flock of blackbirds covering an entire treetop, the tops of several trees, all singing? Suddenly, at exactly the same moment, there's a fluttering of wings and they all soar into the air at once. Above the racket, there must have been some signal, and they all heard it."

"Of course, I've seen that."

"I'm a seaman, and I know that a school of whales playing on the surface of the water, with the curve of the earth between them, will sometimes dive simultaneously. The signal has sounded, but it is too deep for us on deck to hear, although we may feel the vibrations."

"And that is what you think about the voice in the Pirate's House?"

"I only know that there are sounds that most human beings can't hear. The pitch is too high or too low, or, perhaps, too far away in time." Bart reached for his watch and then rose. "I've enjoyed my supper, but now I must go."

"I wonder if there are things that human beings can't see, too?" said Marion.

But Bart was gone.

The Pirate's House, now a famous restaurant, is located at 20 East Broad at Bay Street in Savannah, Georgia. It is surrounded by a ten-acre historic area. The Herb House, said to be the oldest building in Georgia, is part of the complex. For reservations, call (912) 233-5757.

THE GHOSTLY GREETER

Lucas Tavern, Montgomery, Alabama

Old North Hull Street Historic District in Montgomery, Alabama, has a haunted house for a welcome center. How appropriate that it is the home of a ghost said to be unusually cordial.

The most frequent accounts of seeing this ghost—the friendly Eliza Lucas—come from people who pass the house at night and see a woman, dressed in the style of the early nineteenth century, waving at them from the doorway of the Lucas Tavern. Rather than be rude, most wave back and begin to wonder about her only later, especially if the hour is approaching midnight.

In the 1820s Lucas Tavern offered travelers a comfortable place with clean beds, warm victuals, and a friendly hostess. Undoubtedly, one of the great moments of Eliza Lucas's life was when she opened the door to welcome the handsome, bewigged General Lafayette, French hero of the American Revolution, on his visit to Montgomery in 1825. There is no record of what Mrs. Lucas served for dinner that night, but a menu of the tavern fare, found later, listed "chicken pie, ham, five vegetables, pudding and sauce, sweet pies, preserved fruits, a dessert of strawberries and plums, and wine and brandy." All this cost the traveler seventy-five cents.

Those who doubt that Eliza's spirit is at the tavern may begin to believe it after hearing of one Saturday morning in the fall of 1985, when a man arrived, unsolicited, to meet Eliza. He encountered her just inside the front door of the tavern, describing her as of medium height—about five feet three inches tall—and with a warm, pleasant disposition. Strangely enough, the tavern cat, ordinarily very docile, "refuses to go in or out the front door of the tavern unless one of us goes with her, and even then appears uneasy," said Director Mary Ann Neeley. It is a well-known fact that animals often sense the presence of a spirit even when people do not.

The tavern restoration was completed in 1979, and on January 2, 1980, it became the Visitor's Reception Center and home of the offices for the Historic District. "Soon after we occupied it, Eliza began to make her presence felt," said Ms. Neeley.

"In the winter of 1980, there was a late-afternoon meeting in front of the fire in the Tavern Room. The question was controversial, and one person began to speak very heatedly. At that point a great puff of smoke and ashes erupted from the fireplace, covering the dissident with a coat of chimney soot. All we could think of was that Eliza had not agreed with the speaker and had expressed herself forcefully.

"On another occasion two staff members were sitting at a table having lunch and were discussing the Historic District and its operation. With no warning, the door to the room began to just slide off its hinges. As they watched, it continued to slide and finally struck the floor with a resounding thud. Again, Eliza had manifested her displeasure over something that had been said.

"Objects disappear, only to reappear in new locations," Ms. Neeley concluded. "Eliza rearranges, straightens, messes things up, or leaves them about in a quite unpredictable fashion. Nor can we be sure where she will reappear next."

The Hull restoration and its nineteenth-century buildings bring the past to life and is highly popular with visitors, some of whom are amateur photographers.

Vince Ives was one of these. In the late summer of 1986, he

coaxed a hostess into letting him stay to shoot some pictures after the restoration was closed for the day.

When the last visitor had left, and the tour guides as well, Vince went out through the Lucas Tavern's back door and into the square with the other nineteenth-century buildings. They were bathed in the wonderful, warm light of late afternoon. He knew that it would not last long, and he moved quickly from one building to another, shooting.

The third building was the 1890 schoolhouse, one of Vince's favorites. It was filled with all the materials a student would have found in a classroom of the 1800s. Earlier he had noticed its interesting details—the potbellied stove, the pine schoolmaster's desk, the kerosene lamp, the abacus, and the slates. It would have been nice to leave this building until last, like a dessert, but the natural light inside the room would be gone soon, and Vince did not want to use a flash.

He started toward the schoolhouse, thinking he might want to place some "school days" objects on the windowsill for a still arrangement. It would be great to have a teacher or someone using a slate or abacus to photograph in there, but that was out of the question. Vince had a sense of awe as he thought about all the boys and girls who had sat at these desks long ago, students who had grown up and left their mark in the world but who had now been dead for many more years than they had even been alive.

Closing the door quietly behind him, Vince looked around the room to decide where he would begin. Then he started in surprise. All the guides must not have gone, for there sat one in her nineteenth-century costume. She could be a picture subject for him, perhaps pose as the teacher. She was near the window and seemed absorbed in a book with a blue cover. Why had she stayed on after all the others had left?

Wearing that old-fashioned dress, with the light coming in from

The old schoolhouse in the Old North Hull Street Historic District, where the ghostly Eliza once posed for a photographer

the window beside her, she would make a great picture. Vince started to ask her permission, but then thought how ridiculous that was, because none of the guides minded having their pictures taken. Besides, she might change position, and she was perfect just the way she was. Very quietly and unobtrusively, he began to shoot, moving a little to this side or that, adjusting the lens, bracketing. Unfortunately, the tripod he was carrying struck the leg of a desk with a sharp crack, and the sound seemed to startle her. Hurriedly, she got up to leave.

"Wait! Don't go, please. I wonder if I could shoot a picture or two of you there at the old schoolmaster's desk? It won't take long." She did not reply, which seemed rude, and, instead of going toward the desk to sit down, she stopped under the picture of George Washington.

Oh, no, thought Vince. He might be able to get her to pose there under the portrait, but it was too high to show over her head. The picture of her sitting at the desk absorbed in the book would have looked much more natural, as it really might have come from out of the past.

"Pardon me, ma'am. I'm Vince . . ." Then his heart began to pound and his lips refused to form the words he was about to say. As he stood there in the middle of the schoolroom, ready to coax his subject into sitting over at the desk, she reached the picture of Washington. For the first time she appeared to acknowledge Vince's presence, and she turned to wave at him slowly and deliberately. The eyes in the face never really seemed to react to him as a person, although they appeared to stare directly at his face. It was a hot August day in Montgomery, but as Vincent looked back at her, he was chilled to the bone. Then, to his great astonishment, she simply floated right through the wall beneath George Washington's portrait, as effortlessly as if she were passing through an open door.

"Ma'am, ma'am . . . ," he tried to call out, to summon her back.

But words failed him, and, beginning to tremble all over, he sat down in the front row of desks. He stared at the area under the portrait. Then he arose and, walking over to the portrait, ran his fingers over the wall beneath it as he searched for some sign of a door or secret panel that would press inward. He couldn't accept the fact that the girl had simply disappeared. It was almost dark outside when he finally decided to leave. A little dizzy, his knees still weak, Vince walked over to the desk where she had been sitting. On it was an abacus that looked as if it were being used for arithmetic. The blue book that she had been holding was a *McGuffey Reader,* written in the mid-1800s for children.

Later Vince asked Mrs. Neely if Eliza was ever seen in other places besides the front of the tavern.

"Her spirit, you mean? Oh, my goodness, yes. She's a lively one, if you'll pardon the pun. She's been seen in many different buildings here at the restoration, most often the schoolhouse. I doubt if she was ever able to get much formal education in her time, coming from a humble background. But if there was ever anyone who would have wanted to better herself, it was Eliza Lucas. She was ambitious and a hard worker.

"We all feel Eliza's presence, and even while I talk about her now, I think she is trying to tell me how I should present her story," said Ms. Neeley. "The question is, why does Eliza's spirit continue to visit the tavern? My idea is that Eliza, having lived and operated the tavern for more than twenty years, found her most fulfilling moments in this building. It was here that she reared her family and was recognized far and wide as a hostess. We are very fond of Eliza, and I believe she is of us.

"I'll bet she's around here somewhere right now. Wouldn't it be something if you could get a picture of her! Why, Mr. Ives, you look white as a sheet. Are you feeling all right?"

"Yes, of course."

"Mr. Ives, what is that book at your feet?"

Vince stooped down, and, as he looked at the book, his heart began beating madly. It was the *McGuffey Reader*. He read the child's name on the flyleaf, the same name he had seen earlier on the reader in the schoolhouse! How did it get here? It was almost as if Eliza were giving him her "calling card."

"A book on the floor, eh? That's our Eliza, at it again. Did you get some good pictures?"

"I hope so."

"Do come back and see us, Mr. Ives. We want to welcome you just the way Eliza would have done if she were here."

As soon as Vince returned to his car, he unloaded the film he had shot in the schoolroom and marked the top of the can "Eliza." He sent the roll off to Kodak when he returned home, not trusting it to a local processor. When he picked it up and put the slides on his lightbox, the pictures of the buildings were fine, as were those of the exterior of the schoolhouse. But all the frames that he had shot inside were blank, except for showing a streak of bright, golden light over at the left or the middle or the right, never in the same place, but "depending on where 'Eliza' was standing as I moved around framing my picture," he said to himself wonderingly, as he looked at his slides.

All Vince needed to do now was to find a photography book with instructions for the proper exposure to capture both the man-made backdrop of a schoolroom and a good sharp image of a ghost.

Lucas Tavern is in the Old North Hull Street Historic District, open Monday through Saturday from 9:30 A.M. to 4:00 P.M. and Sunday from 1:30 to 3:30 P.M. There is an admission fee. For more information, write 310 North Hull Street, Montgomery, Alabama 36104, or call (334) 262–0322.

BEWARE THE LIGHTS OF LOUDOUN

Loudoun House, Philadelphia, Pennsylvania

It was in the early 1940s, just after Miss Maria Dickinson Logan died, and yet I remember it as clearly as though it was only a few months ago. My wife, Elizabeth, and I occupied a room in the house while I was looking after the place. I don't think either of us will ever forget the nights we spent there, when I was a temporary caretaker.

If you are familiar with Loudoun, you know that it is the house with four white columns across the front and that it stands at the top of Neglee's Hill, where Germantown Avenue passes Apsley Street. Miss Logan willed the house to the City of Philadelphia to be maintained as a museum.

One night, about the middle of December, my wife was awakened by a feeling of intense cold and the sense of a strong breeze blowing full on her face. She sat up in bed and saw to her great amazement a tall column of cloudy white light extending from the foot of the bed straight up to the ceiling. Staring at it spellbound, she noticed that the light fell across the bed so that she could see the pattern of the spread; it also illuminated the dressing table and mirror. She was extremely frightened, pulled the covers up over her head, and lay there petrified. Eventually, she gathered enough courage to look out; when she did the room was completely dark.

When I woke up Elizabeth described the column of light to me. I could hardly believe this, and she was worried that I might think it was either a dream or something that had occurred in a half-wakeful state. But she seemed so certain that I told her to awaken me immediately if she saw the luminous column again.

A few weeks later I woke up early in the morning to find her calling to me.

"Hurry! I want you to see it."

"See what?" I was still half asleep.

"That thing is here again."

I rose up in bed and looked in every direction, but the room was extremely dark, and I saw no sign of light. We then turned on the lamp, and my wife said that while I was asleep, just before she woke me up, there had been a bright, globular light at the foot of the bed. At first it was the size of a child's rubber ball, and then it began to increase in size until it must have been three feet in diameter and was taller than the bed. Again, there was a filmy appearance, and the inside glowed as if there were a light in it.

She had tried to awaken me but could only elicit a groan, as I seemed to be in a deep slumber. All the while the light was directly at my feet and partly over the edge of the bed. Afraid that it might grow into something dangerous, Elizabeth shook me vigorously. The light kept on shining and growing larger, but when I finally did wake up and answer her, she said that it collapsed at once and sank down into strange-looking folds, similar to those of an accordion. This time I took her story much more seriously, and, after I turned out the lamp, we watched together until daybreak. The light did not reappear.

I was walking back to Loudoun one day when a neighborhood boy stopped me for a few minutes to talk. It seems he delivered newspapers early in the morning, and on several occasions in the winter, while it was still dark, he had seen lights flashing on the

Loudoun House, built on a hill over the bodies of Revolutionary War soldiers, has its own strange story.

darkened front windows of the house. I think he really wanted to know whether I had seen anything. I didn't let on that my wife had.

Elizabeth and I both came to share the feeling that there was a presence in the house. Whether it was that of Miss Maria Logan or her brother, who lived here with her for many years, or even some earlier owner, we had no way of knowing. My wife thought it was Miss Logan, and sometimes, when she would find a book or magazine out of place, she would say, "I wonder if this is something Miss Logan was reading." When she would say that, it always gave me an eerie feeling.

A month or so must have passed, and we had begun to think that whatever had happened was an isolated event and would occur no more. Then, late in the summer, I woke up to my Elizabeth's hand gently pressing my shoulder and her whisper, "It's here."

"What is it?" I asked. I rose to a sitting position, and there, at the end of the bed before me, was an awesome cloud of glowing light about four feet in diameter, suspended in the air. It was only a few feet away. As I watched it began to float upward like a gas-filled balloon, and I thought that it would hit the ceiling. It seemed to go straight up, but when it reached the ceiling, rather than stopping, it went right through it. I know I cried out, but it was an exclamation of wonder rather than of fear.

I checked the room to see if light was coming in from any source, and there was none. Passing the door, I tried the night latch and found it secure. I said to Elizabeth, "Tell me from the beginning what you saw."

"I first woke up when I felt the bed vibrate due to a shock, which may have been under it, or it may have come from someone striking the surface of the bed," she said. "There at the foot sat an elderly woman in a white dress, looking very calm. Her clenched fist rested on the footboard, and I had the feeling that she had just hit the bed. She sat there bathed in light, a light so bright that it illuminated the room. I tried to wake you, and when you first spoke, the figure began to dissolve into the luminous cloud. First the head went, then the body, and a moment later the cloud drifted up to the ceiling and disappeared." The last part of her story was exactly what I had seen myself.

On the next occasion the figure of the woman stood by my side as I slept. My wife roused me, and as I woke up, it vanished with a flash of light as bright as the flare of a match.

After my wife and I left Loudoun, for our services were no longer needed, we came back a few years later and stopped to talk with the caretaker. He had seen lights on several occasions but never anything as distinct or as close to him as Elizabeth and I had experienced.

Mrs. John W. Farr, who was head of the Friends of Loudoun, relates, "Some of the neighbors say that Miss Logan is guarding the property. Children tell of seeing someone sitting on the sunporch, most often a little old lady. And, I must say, a number of things have happened for which there are no explanations."

On one occasion Mrs. Farr's committee members arranged some heirloom plates in a china closet in Loudoun House. Returning several days later to continue their work, they found that there were no plates in the china closet. The plates eventually turned up on such a high shelf that it took a ladder to reach them. Both the china closet in which the plates had been arranged and the house itself had been securely locked.

When she was ready to leave the house one day, Mrs. Farr discovered that the large pocketbook she had left in the drawing room was missing. A search through the house proved fruitless. Two days later, though, there was the bag, in plain view in another room. Nothing was missing from it.

Dick Nicolai, Fairmount Park Promotion Director, has heard a story over the years that might account for the missing bag. A playful ghost called Willie, a member of the Armat family who died quite young, is said to return and move small objects about.

The live-in caretaker has never had a problem with break-ins, and neither did the caretaker before him, who was on the premises for twenty-seven years. That record is unusual. But it is possible that fewer people try to break into houses said to be haunted.

Might more than one spirit live on Neglee's Hill? During the Battle of Germantown in November of 1777 wounded American soldiers were carried to the top of the hill on which Loudoun now stands. Many were dead or dying. Some were removed in wagons to Philadelphia, but some—not even dead, just comatose—were buried there while they were yet alive. Is it possible that, when winter winds make dried leaves rustle, the restless spirits of those unfortunate young men rise and walk again?

Loudoun was built by Thomas Armat in 1801. He named it after the county in Virginia from which he had come. The house is reminiscent of those of Virginia, and he must have had many pleasant memories of his early years in the South. Armat, a distinguished philanthropist and a man of strong faith and inventive mind, was one of the founders of St. Luke's Episcopal Church. The house museum, containing much of the home's original furniture, is open to visitors on Sunday afternoons. It is located at the northwest corner of Germantown Avenue and Apsley Street, in the historic Germantown section of Philadelphia, Pennsylvania. Lightning caused a fire in 1993, and the house is undergoing restoration. Further information may be obtained by calling the Fairmount Parks Commission at (215) 686–1776.

THE HERMITAGE

Near Myrtle Beach, South Carolina

There are few people alive or dead who are more famous in South Carolina than lovely young Alice Flagg. She once lived at a house called The Hermitage in Murrell's Inlet. The number of visitors to her grave is amazing, since it was more than a century ago that the sixteen-year-old Alice went to school in Charleston, studied, danced, fell passionately in love, and died a tragic death.

Generations of young people have visited Alice's grave under the moss-draped oaks at All Saints Waccamaw Church. To this day, people say that the ghost of Alice still appears at the cemetery and roams the marshes of Murrell's Inlet.

Dr. Allard Belin Flagg built the house in 1848, choosing a point of land surrounded on three sides by tidal marshes. He placed it within a grove of live oaks that at that time were at least one hundred years old. They are still in the spot where The Hermitage once stood. A new development is being built here currently. Although it was never a *Gone With the Wind*-style antebellum home, the first impression of The Hermitage was of a house with character and serenity on a green lawn and surrounded by huge oaks. Across the front porch were immense white columns, each carved from a single tree.

Reilly Burns, a serious young engineer who visited the house from out of state, related his own experience.

The Hermitage at Murrell's Inlet, near Myrtle Beach, is haunted by one of the state's most famous ghosts.

Often after my arrival in Myrtle Beach, the story of Alice would come up, and each time I would make a skeptical or sarcastic comment. Finally, I decided to investigate for myself and see if there really was an apparition of a girl named Alice.

When I arrived at The Hermitage, the Willcoxes welcomed me as cordially as if I had been an invited guest rather than someone who had arrived unannounced. Clarke Willcox and his wife, Lillian, were warmly hospitable and seemed to enjoy showing me around the house. The flooring of beautiful twenty-foot lengths of heart pine and dowel trim, expertly done by slaves, decorates the front parlor. Upstairs over the front porch is an unusual round-hinged window with curved spokes and a central eye.

"She probably looked out that window many a time, for that was Alice's bedroom," said Clarke Willcox, gesturing toward the room on my right as I stood with my back to the round window. The room was white, as was the spread on the spool bed. Over a door hung a needlework sampler upon which had been worked, in large letters, the name "Alice." It was a room that might have been typical of any young girl before the Civil War, what with its dainty, ruffled curtains, its innocence, its simplicity.

We sat down on the porch and continued to talk about the house. The front steps and walk are of sturdy English ballast brick, used to prevent light sailboats from capsizing in mid-ocean. When not needed, these bricks were often thrown into harbors and rivers, and many of them, when retrieved, paved the streets of Charleston and Savannah. It appeared that Mr. Willcox was not going to bring up the subject of Alice, which I had been prepared to ask questions about—questions that, in the light of my hosts' obvious intelligence and culture, now seemed somewhat rude.

"Everyone who comes here probably asks you to tell them the story about Alice," I finally said, leading into the subject in a manner that I felt did not indicate either belief or unbelief.

"You're right," my host replied, "and with so many questions about the story, I suppose that I have thought about her almost daily during the years we have lived in the house. No description of The Hermitage would really be complete without the tragedy of Alice Flagg. I gather you wish to hear it?" I nodded, and Mr. Willcox began his story.

"Alice was the sixteen-year-old sister of Dr. Allard Belin Flagg, who built The Hermitage. Since there was a considerable age difference between Allard and his younger sister, and since their father was dead, Allard always dominated his sister. He was more like a parent than a brother, and at times a tyrannical and disapproving parent at that.

"On her last vacation at home from finishing school in Charleston, Alice wore her new engagement ring on a ribbon around her neck beneath her blouse, unable to brave Allard's rage if he saw it. She did everything possible to conceal even her happiness, for she was aware of his contempt for a man who was in the turpentine industry, a mere merchant, rather than a member of the professional or planter class.

"She returned to school after Christmas, and that spring was one of joy and secret planning for the future with her fiance. The high point of the social season each year was the Spring Ball, at which the debutantes were presented. Alice made her debut in the most beautiful white gown imaginable. Those who saw her commented on how lovely she looked and on the becoming color in her cheeks as she danced one dance after another with her fiance. Her mother was not able to attend for she had fled from the Low Country, with its dreaded malaria season, to the mountains. Fortunately, young Allard was not present either, too busy visiting patients and operating the farm.

"The day following the ball, Alice was suddenly stricken with the fever prevalent in the area. School authorities sent for Dr. Flagg. After equipping the family carriage with medications and articles for Alice's comfort, he set out with a servant over the miserable roads to Charleston. It was a four-day one-way trip from Murrell's Inlet, and there were five rivers to ford.

"When they arrived back at The Hermitage, Dr. Flagg was able to give his young sister a more thorough examination, and, in doing so, he found the engagement ring. Allard snatched it from her neck with such force that the ribbon broke. Then he strode outdoors and threw the ring into the creek. Alice was broken-hearted, and when visitors would come to her sickroom, she would beg them to find her ring. Her distress was apparent to all, and finally a young cousin went to Georgetown and bought a ring. When he pressed it into her hand, weak and near death as she was, she knew the difference. She threw it on the floor and begged him to find *her* ring.

"One week after her arrival at home, Alice breathed her last. There was not sufficient time for her mother even to get back from the mountains before the casket was closed, and Alice was buried temporarily in the yard of The Hermitage. When her mother returned, the girl's body was moved to the family plot at All Saints Waccamaw Church, on the river opposite Pawley's Island. Beneath the beautiful trees in the old cemetery and amid the imposing stones raised in memory of the other Flaggs may be seen a flat, white-marble slab. Upon it is engraved the single word ALICE.

"It is an epitaph telling in its simplicity. It would be given only to one who was unknown save for her first name—or so loved that only the first name was needed. I have walked through that cemetery many a time and seen a vase of flowers on her grave, a tribute to her left by some unknown donor. People are very romantic, aren't they?" Mr. Willcox commented.

"Do you think that Alice really does come back?" I asked him.

"People have been seeing the ghost of Alice Flagg for a hundred years or more. They were seeing it when I was a boy," was his reply.

"When she appears, what does she do?"

"Old people in the area say that she searches for her ring and that her spirit won't rest until she finds it."

"Does she ever come back here to the house?"

"My wife and I have often felt her presence in her bedroom. An aunt of mine slept in that room while I was growing up. One day, when she was looking in the mirror and brushing her hair, she suddenly saw a lovely girl in a white dress reflected in the mirror beside her. She turned, and no one was there. Aunt Emma screamed all the way down the stairs," he said, chuckling.

"Then there are some who claim to have conjured up her ghost in the cemetery." Mr. Willcox stared thoughtfully out over the salt marshes. "Some nights I think she is out there or even under the trees on the lawn, searching for the ring, never giving up her quest. I've looked for it myself, but if I ever found it, I wouldn't know what to do with it. How could I get it back to her?"

"Where is Alice's grave located in the cemetery?" I asked.

"Beyond the church on the right. You're going out there, aren't you?"

"I probably will." The sun had set by now, and it was getting chilly on the porch. We both stood up, and I thanked Mr. Willcox for his kindness.

It was time for dinner, and I looked forward to eating at Oliver's or one of the other seafood restaurants on Highway 17. I thought it would be best for me to go out to the cemetery in the morning. The meal was delicious, but as I ate I became more and more tempted to find Alice's grave that night. If the moon was out, it might be possible; if not, there was no hope at all in the darkness.

The sky was clouded over, and there was no sign of the moon or even a star. I drove south on Highway 17, and somehow, seemingly without even being able to help it, my car turned right and took the road to All Saints Waccamaw Cemetery. I had a powerful flashlight in the trunk that I could shine on some of the stones, but trying to find her slab that night was risky.

By the time I pulled up and stopped beside the old cemetery, I was beginning to feel foolish. If anyone passed and saw my light bobbing about out there, would they think I was a vandal, perhaps even a grave robber? Ahead were the gates. Would they be locked? They opened easily, I found; and as I went in, I closed and latched them carefully. Where had Mr. Willcox said her grave was?

Somewhere beyond the church . . . past the front steps and then to the right? Was that where he had meant?

I shone my light on one of the stones, but it was not a member of the Flagg family. Off in the distance, a dog howled mournfully. Wasn't that considered an omen of death? I didn't know whether I was nervous or just felt foolish being here on such a mission. Sometimes I bumped into markers, and that gave me a real start. At other times I would step on a sunken grave and feel my feet sink still further into the soft, sandy soil.

For more than thirty minutes I must have wandered about the cemetery, with no success. It is not easy to find a flat stone at night. And then I stepped on it. When I did, I jumped to one side, for the act of standing on someone's gravestone seemed sacrilegious. I shone the light down squarely on the white marble, and there, engraved in large letters, was the name ALICE. My excitement was so great that I dropped the light, and as it hit the stone, it went out. It didn't really matter, though, because I had found her grave. With my index finger I traced the letters. It was the stone I had been looking for!

Someone had said that teenagers often come out here at night and walk around the grave thirteen times, hoping to commune with Alice's spirit. At least there was none of that foolishness going on tonight, for I seemed to be the only one in the cemetery. I had taken a picture of The Hermitage and wanted to take a picture of the stone—just as a curiosity, of course. But I could come back here in the morning before I left and do that. It was getting quite misty, and even a flash shot might not turn out well.

"What are you doing down there on the ground?" asked a feminine voice.

I turned around. Behind me stood a girl who must have come up without my hearing her. It was probably one of the teenagers who often visited the gravesite.

"I was looking for the grave of a girl named Alice."

"You have found it," she replied.

"Do you come here often?"

"Oh, I'm out here quite a lot, most often when some of my friends are out at night, too."

"Isn't it pretty foolish for you and your friends to come out here in this old cemetery to see the grave of a girl who has been dead more than a hundred years?"

"You make that sound like a very long time."

"Isn't it?"

"It doesn't seem long to me at all."

As she talked, I thought her dress appeared almost luminous. The moonlight must have been shining on it. I looked up at the sky, and the moon was out for the first time that night.

"Why did you come out here?" asked the girl.

"I suppose I wanted to know if all the stories I had heard were true and if there really was such a thing as the spirit of a beautiful girl named Alice."

"What a ridiculous question."

My heart began to hammer. "Do you mean you are Alice?"

Her white raiment was glowing even brighter until I could scarcely look at it.

"Of course I am Alice, and my home is The Hermitage."

"Then what are you doing here in this cemetery?" I asked more boldly, but she ignored my question.

"Did you come to help me?"

"That depends. What would you like for me to do?"

"I want you to help me find my ring. I've been looking for it ever so long."

"I'm not sure I can do that. Your brother threw it away, you know."

"How could he do something so wicked? Where is it?"

While she talked, her dress became so bright that I had to turn my eyes away. A cloud of mist came rolling up from the river and enveloped us. As we entered the cloud, for the first time I was afraid.

"If I ever see Allard Flagg, I will surely tell him . . . ," she was saying, and her voice faded. When the cloud finally passed, the girl was gone, and so was the moon. I heard the angry rumble of thunder in the distance, the prelude to a coming storm.

For the first time in my life, I found myself trembling violently. My eyes had been exposed to such brilliant light that they were not readjusting well, and the darkness of the cemetery was overwhelming.

What had happened to the practical, down-to-earth engineer whom I had always considered myself to be? Without my flashlight, how would I find the gate? Suddenly, I heard a metallic clang, and I realized that someone had closed the gate noisily. Was I imagining that I heard the rattle of a chain securing it? Had a night watchman locked me in?

In my haste to get out, I stumbled over a footstone and barely managed to keep from falling. I stretched my arm out in front of me for some protection, and my fingers rested on a clammy marble face. Whether the face was that of an angel or Christ, I was not sure, for I didn't leave my hand there long enough to find out. Finally, I managed to make my way to the gate. I reached for the latch automatically and when I did, I discovered that I could have walked right through it. Instead of being closed, the gate was ajar. What about the sound I had just heard? Hadn't I been careful to latch it behind me? Yes, I was certain I had.

Reilly Burns has become a believer, I thought to myself as I drove down Highway 17 north toward Myrtle Beach. That night I lay on the bed in my motel room, hands clasped behind my head. I thought for a long, long time of a girl named Alice whom I would never see again—at least not on this earth.

———————————————

The Hermitage was moved recently from its location at Murrell's Inlet to make way for a housing development. A new site has not yet been determined.

HOUSE OF TRAGEDY

Carnton Plantation, Franklin, Tennessee

"There will never be another Carnton House," his friend had said. "Never a place that's seen such tragedy and grief."

Perhaps that was the reason Paul Levitt was determined to go there. Up the curving drive, set far back from the road, the house stood alone in a grove of maple trees, its darkened windows staring out from between tall, white columns. There was something lonely and mysterious about it.

November 30th had been one of those timeless autumn days, but now it was late afternoon, with darkness falling fast. As Paul drove up to the house in his black Ferrari, he realized that he had arrived too late. It was just after five, and the tour guides would already have left. Well, it didn't matter; he would walk about the grounds. All was quiet. He and this house were alone in another world. The only sound was the faint crunching of his footsteps on the gravel drive. It was a time to think and to absorb the unfathomable atmosphere of this place that his friend John Carter had described.

Underfoot, a profusion of leaves lay like a golden treasure spread out by some profligate Midas. It seemed almost wrong to tread upon such beauty. Bending down, Paul picked up one perfect, five-pointed yellow maple leaf, then another; but on the second leaf were splotches of crimson, bright as blood.

It reminded him of how many men had suffered and died here.

Carnton House is probably Tennessee's best-known haunted house.

What was it his great-grandmother in Ohio once said? Something like, "Your great-grandaddy fought in a terrible battle at a place called Franklin." He was walking over the same ground where his ancestor had fought. Wasn't it a strange coincidence that today was the anniversary of that struggle? It had lasted just five hours, but what a bloody, disastrous battle it had been.

Paul walked without considering the time, for he was in no hurry to return to the motel. He found the pressures of his work beginning to leave him. Almost automatically, his feet followed a path that led from the house across the fields. Where was he going? Did it matter?

Finally, the path brought him around to the back of the house, and near the porch he saw the figure of a man getting on a horse. If the fellow paused, Paul decided he would speak to him. On second thought, he would take the initiative and hail him.

"Hello, there. Nice horse."

"Yep. Had my own horse shot from under me. But I suppose it doesn't matter. Whether you ride or whether you go on foot, you are still at their mercy tonight."

This was strange talk. Paul wasn't frightened, but he did find himself tingling slightly.

The man spoke again. "If you're coming with me, you had better find a pistol or a carbine; otherwise you won't last long out there. But not many of us will live through tonight, anyway."

What was he talking about? thought Paul, now close enough to see the man fairly well. He had a mustache, a short beard, and eyes that bored straight through you, and he sat there in the afterdusk, humming to himself.

"We are a band of brothers and native to the soil, hm, hm, hm, hmm . . . And when our rights were threatened, the cry rose near and far, hurray, for the Bonnie Blue Flag that bears a single star."

Good lord, thought Paul, they must be having one of those battle reenactments out there today, and this fellow thinks that I am part of it. From his dress, Paul assumed that the man was an officer. His hat was black cloth with small gilt buttons on the sides; strands of gold braid met in the front in a four-leaf clover without a stem. He wore it with the leather visor pulled down, almost as if he were trying to protect his face. At his belt were not only a carbine and pistol but a stout sword as well.

"What kind of carbine is that you're wearing?"

"It's an Enfield .577. What do you have?"

"Me? Nothing. Man, I've just seen them in books. I never shot one, or a pistol, either. A sword? I wouldn't know what to do with that."

The stranger raised his eyebrows in surprise. "You had better go over to the Carter house then, or into town. This is no place for you tonight. That fool Hood thinks he's as brilliant as Lee, but he's sending my men to be slaughtered!"

Then he seemed to be talking to someone by his side. The officer's voice rose in anger. "They have three lines of works, and they are all completed."

If there was a reply, Paul didn't hear it. But he did hear the officer's voice once more, and above the rustle of autumn leaves, the words floated back to him strong and clear.

"Well, Govan, if we are to die, let us die like men!"

With that, Paul saw the stranger, who had never bothered to introduce himself, fling his cap furiously into the air and then ride off. From the distance came the shout, "Charge men! Charge! Do you hear me, do you hear . . . " And the sound of the voice faded away in a maelstrom of shot and shell, musketry and cannon. Then smoke, or was it mist, seemed to lie all about him. Paul thought he heard a regiment band strike up the strains of "Annie Laurie."

A few seconds later came the most awesome sound that Paul had ever heard. A veritable chorus of men's voices shattered the air with the fierce, bloodcurdling attack cry that Union troops had soon learned was the Rebel Yell.

Paul Levitt did what many raw recruits had done when they heard that yell: He began to run. As he ran, his heart pounded. He seemed to be surrounded by the fire of thousands of small arms and the roar of shells. Death pervaded the very atmosphere. He thought he was heading back to his car but, losing his sense of direction, he found himself stumbling about in the graveyard not far from the house. It was a cemetery provided by Carnton shortly after the battle, for a day later more than 1,700 Confederate men lay dead in the fields near this home.

Finally, Paul made his way back to his car. What was it his

friend Carter had said? That "on this ground the rows of dead once stood six men deep, so close they could not fall."

Paul slept poorly, for all night long he dreamed that he was in the midst of one furious charge after another. But early the next morning, he was out at the house again. If he had been part of some supernatural experience or seen a ghost, as he believed he had, he wanted to understand it.

He was fortunate to arrive on a day when Bernice Seiberling was there. Mrs. Seiberling, a delightful, gray-haired lady with a thorough knowledge of the history of Carnton, had long been guiding visitors through the house.

"I would imagine that a house with this much history has some ghost stories connected with it," Paul said tentatively, as a way to introduce the subject.

"Oh my, yes," said Mrs. Seiberling, not reluctant to share stories of some of the spirits. And she began to talk about a former cook at Carnton during Civil War days and the ghost's ways of getting attention.

"I had been aware of her for quite a while, for I would hear glasses clinking in the kitchen as if someone were washing dishes. Than I began to hear her in other areas of the house. One day I had a tour going, and it sounded as if rocks were being thrown at the windows and breaking them.

"Most of the noises were coming from one room. When we reached it, we found a framed picture of the house lying face up on top of the heater, its glass shattered in a million pieces. It was as though someone had carefully placed it there. One of the men on the tour took his camera and made a picture of it, for, he said, 'It's impossible for that picture to have fallen in such a way.'

"On another occasion," Mrs. Sieberling continued, "I was here alone on a cold winter day and kept hearing a noise in a small enclosed porch at the back of the house, so I went to investigate.

We keep a box of old glass panes on a shelf there. I found two panes of the thin old glass, unbroken, one lying on each side of the door. The box, of course, was still on the shelf. It's as though the spirit has a sense of humor and likes to play tricks on me. We had all heard things but had no idea what was causing them until one day a descendant of the Carnton family said, 'You know there was a murder in this house, don't you?'

"It seems that one of the field hands murdered a young girl in the kitchen in the early 1840s or before, probably due to some motive such as jealousy. There was prejudice on the part of house servants toward those who did the heavy work on the plantation, and the girl may have rejected the field hand or had another sweetheart.

"Sometimes it sounds exactly like dishes are being washed. One night ten of us were all in the dining room having our regular board meeting of the Carnton Society. The lady sitting beside me turned to me and said, 'I think I hear someone in the kitchen.' I just answered, 'No.' She turned to me again in a few minutes and said, 'I know someone is in there,' and this time I said, 'There is no one in the kitchen.' But she got up and went back there.

"When she returned and sat down, she had the strangest expression on her face. 'You're right,' she said, 'no one is there.' I told the other members of the board about hearing the cook and her antics, and they believed me. Even many visitors who come here ask me if we have spirits in the house. It amazes me that strangers seem to feel it, although when there are lots of workmen around, we don't hear the spirits as much.

"A workman told me he saw a beautiful girl with dark hair in the upstairs hall. His eyes were huge, and his face was white; he won't work up there now unless someone is with him. Whether she was one of the two surviving Carnton children who had grown into womanhood that he saw or not, I don't know. The Carntons lost three children out of five in infancy. That seems shocking to us, but many people didn't even live to middle age a hundred or so years ago."

Paul had begun to doubt that he would hear any story relating to his own experience, when finally Mrs. Seiberling changed the subject.

"I hope you won't think I am silly when I tell you something else that has been reported to us here. Visitors say they have seen a Confederate soldier who walks the perimeter of this property. I don't laugh at them anymore, for there have been times in the late afternoon, especially in fall, when I have heard my own ghost soldier or, should I say, the sound of heavy footsteps. When I hear those striding feet, I hurry to look out, but the back veranda is always empty.

"This house was used as a hospital after the Battle of Franklin, and the bodies of four Confederate generals were placed on that back porch. The most loved general was the Irishman Pat Cleburne, and all the next day, men who had survived the battle filed past, paying their last respects to him. It is said that when Cleburne died, the South lost a general second only to Stonewall Jackson. Before he was buried, Mrs. Carrie McGavock, mistress of the plantation, took the general's cap, later presenting it to the State of Tennessee Museum."

"What did the cap look like?" Paul asked.

"It was a round, black cap with little buttons on each side. I don't know how many. And there were strips of gold braid that came up to the front and ran into a four-leaf clover. Poor General Cleburne. They say he was a very brave man."

Black with gold braid, a four-leaf clover—Levitt remembered that cap, and as Mrs. Seiberling went on talking, he missed part of what she was saying about the names of former residents of Carnton.

"People who have lived here and others in the area have reported hearing a Confederate soldier pace to and fro on the front porch. They come back and ask if I have heard him. I tell them, yes, I have heard him many times."

Struck by the similarity of the cap on the officer he had seen and the one belonging to the general, Levitt had heard what he had come to find out. He believed that the stranger he had seen the evening before was none other than the spirit of General Pat Cleburne. But how could he tell Mrs. Seiberling such a story? He simply let her talk on.

"I warn you, this house has a pull about it, and if you ever visit it, you'll come back," said Bernice Seiberling. "People return again and again."

"Return again and again" echoed in Paul's mind. It may be that spirits do, too, he thought.

Carnton is a timeless place. It is a place where "the dead once stood . . . so close they could not fall," where bullets came thick as rain, and where soldiers pulled their caps down over their faces in a desperate, futile attempt to protect themselves. It is a place to shudder at men's ferocity toward other men. It is probably Tennessee's most haunted house.

Carnton Plantation is in Franklin, Tennessee, not far from Nashville. The house is open seven days a week except in January, February, and March, when it is open Monday through Friday. Its twenty-two rooms contain much of the original furnishings, which are from the period 1820 to 1860. All the woodwork is wood-grained to resemble mahogany or rosewood. The house was decorated not long after the excavation of Pompeii, when mustard yellow, soldier blue, and Pompeii red were in vogue.

THE TRAMPING FEET

The Gaffos House, Portsmouth, Virginia

The grizzled old sea captain didn't know when he had prayed last. It must have been many years ago, but it hadn't saved her. His lovely Maureen had died anyway. She had never been a strong one, and when the baby was born and there were complications, she was gone in a day or two. But behind her she left a treasure: tiny Cathy.

Fortunately, his mother had stepped in and taken care of the infant. It was hard to realize that Cathy was now a young girl. For the past two years, since his mother's passing, she had made a home for him. Now he was about to lose her, too.

"God, don't let the girl die. I know I could have been a better man, and I don't deserve her. I never have talked much to you. Maybe I don't know how. But I'm trying, Lord." On he went, up the steps of the four-story house that had been turned into a hospital for Portsmouth's yellow-fever victims. The house was filled with patients, and beds had even been placed in the halls. Cathy was on the fourth floor, and that day she was tossing and turning so much that it made tears run down the old captain's weather-beaten cheeks just to watch her.

He cradled her frail body in his arms, pleading, "I will take you to Richmond and buy you such lovely clothes—everything you want. Look at me; speak to me! Cathy, you must get well, you must," he cried out. But like many other poor souls who were brought to the hospital, turning and tossing in the throes of the virulent yellow fever, Cathy did not get well.

A Portsmouth gentleman who swears that his seagoing grandfather knew the captain says that the captain stayed out at sea as much as he could after Cathy's death. When he returned for brief shore stays, his solitary figure could be seen striding along in front of the homes a few blocks from the water. There he often paused to stare up at the fourth-floor windows of the house at 218 Glasgow Street.

How could so much happen in this cheerful-looking house? It is yellow with blue shutters, and its interior is bright with shades of red, green, and gold. But the house did not always look this attractive. When Mary Alice and George Gaffos were first married, they moved into a ground-floor apartment here, as the old house was then divided into apartments. A full English-basement home, it rises four stories above ground. The couple soon began to dream of buying and restoring it, despite its unhappy history and their modest income.

A few years later, however, they did buy and remodel it. Their dream had come true, but it was not all that they had expected. Or should we say that the house contained more than they expected and could ever have believed?

The Gaffoses are a pleasant, attractive couple. Mary Alice tells the story.

From the first few weeks we lived here, strange things happened. The children noticed it first. Andrea would call us time after time, telling us that she had heard heavy feet going up the stairs. The girls slept on the third floor and were very frightened there for a while. One night Andrea called, and I ran up to her room.

"It was going up the stairs again tonight, Mother," she said. "I could hear the footsteps tramping up each tread, like someone with boots on, and I wondered if those feet were going to stop at

The front door of 218 Glasgow opens during the night, heavy footsteps can be heard going up three flights of stairs, and then the attic door closes.

the top of the stairs on my floor. I just held my breath!"

She threw her arms around my neck and hung on to me for dear life. Then our older girl, Sabrina, chimed in: "They never stop, though. They go right on up to the fourth floor, Mother, and sometimes we can hear them in the attic overhead."

George and I got so frustrated for a while, we really didn't know how to handle it, for we thought the children were just hearing old-house noises. I made up all sorts of funny and comforting stories about the footsteps on the stairs to take their fear away. After a while, they said they weren't afraid anymore.

One winter evening about a year later, my husband and I were sitting in front of the fire, working a jigsaw puzzle. We enjoy doing them and sometimes sit up quite late. I remember that I had just found a piece we had been looking for all evening and was putting it in the right place when—bam! The front door slammed so hard that we both nearly jumped out of our chairs. We sat looking at each other, frozen, waiting to see what would happen next.

Then came a series of thuds that sounded like heavy boots going up the stairs, step by step. We heard them reach the top of the first floor. They went on. When they got to the second floor, George was out of his chair.

"I'm going up there, Mary Alice," he said. The steps seemed to pause at the third-floor landing. Then we heard them again. Now he—if it were a man—was on his way up to the fourth floor.

I was so relieved that he had passed the third floor, until we heard the attic door at the top of the stairs open and slam hard as it shut. George's face was white as he ran out into the hall and up the stairs, with me close behind him. We were very much afraid, and we both wondered what we were going to find in the attic. At the third floor I stopped and switched on the light upstairs, but when we reached the fourth-floor landing, no light at all could be seen under the door.

"I'm not going into a completely dark room. Stay right here," said George. "I'll get the flashlight and be back in a second." It seemed as if he were gone forever, but it probably wasn't over a minute or two until he returned. "Get behind me," he whispered, and I did. He threw open the door and swung the powerful flashlight from one end of the room to the other. The attic was empty! With relief, we both just collapsed into each other's arms.

Nothing happened for about a month after that. Then one night, when George was working on the third floor on something he had brought home from the office and I was reading to Sabrina, he called downstairs.

"What are the girls doing playing in the attic this late?"

"What do you mean?" I asked.

"I hear them walking all over the place up there."

"You couldn't," I said. "Sabrina is down here with me, and Andrea is asleep in her bedroom up there with you." I heard George go into Andrea's room, and in few minutes he came downstairs, carrying the sleeping child in his arms.

"I want you all to get out of the house immediately. There is someone upstairs. Go across the street, and, if you hear a gunshot, call the police."

He searched the attic, looked under beds, and opened closet doors on every floor of the house. But like the night that the two of us had gone up to the attic, there was nothing to be found, at least nothing that anyone could see.

My mother probably had one of the strangest experiences of all. We were going on a business trip, and she volunteered to spend the night with the girls. She slept in our room, which is right between the girls' bedrooms. Just as it does at home, her little dog slept on a pillow beside the bed. In the middle of the night, my mother awoke to a thump, thump, thump. The first thing she thought about was the ghost. She determined that she wasn't frightened and that she was going to see if anything was there.

Thinking it might be her dog, she said, "Susie, now you get right back on the pillow." She reached over and found the dog was there. Then she exclaimed out loud to herself, "My Lord. It's the ghost!"

Her finger flipped the light switch, and, when the light went on, she saw her bedroom slippers being tossed into the air. Up and down and up and down. To her, the bizarre and frightening spectacle seemed to last forever, but it was probably only a few seconds. She didn't get to sleep again until after the sun came up.

Mary Alice Gaffos and her family have lived at 218 Glasgow now for a quarter of a century. "Sometimes months go by and nothing happens. Then we may see our dog looking as if he is ready to spring into space and barking his head off as he faces an empty corner in the front hall. When that happens, we know the captain is back!"

If the daughter of the sea captain really did die in this house during the yellow-fever epidemic, it surely broke the old man's heart. Does his love for her still go on in some timeless dimension? Does it sometimes bring him back?

If you want to visit the site of the haunting, The Gaffos House, located at 218 Glasgow Street, is one of the houses on the Old Portsmouth Halloween Haunted House Tour. The tour takes place every year on the last Friday in October. Everyone meets first at Trinity Episcopal Church at 500 Court Street, Portsmouth, Virginia. The cemetery seems a fitting place to start. This is a popular town, and tickets for the tour are available in August and September; anyone showing up that night without a ticket will be disappointed. For more information, call the church office at (804) 393–0431.

HOW TO KILL A SPY

Seven Stars Tavern, Woodstown, New Jersey

There are houses that have an overwhelming sense of mystery, houses that reach out and capture your imagination by evoking thoughts of the spirits of people who have lived within their walls. For me, there was just such a house.

Years ago, when I was a child living in Woodstown, New Jersey, I would pass it on sunny days and rainy days alike. Sometimes I would see it looming up darkly beside the road, wrapped in dense fog common to this low-lying area. But whatever the weather, I invariably felt the house's spell. Named Seven Stars Tavern, it was built in 1762 at the intersection of Kings Highway and the Woodstown–Auburn Road.

Many stories of the supernatural are connected with Seven Stars, but space here allows for only the most famous one. It is the story of the ghost of a Tory spy. The event upon which it is based is said to be a historical fact. According to the owner, Robert Brooks, a man loyal to the British during the Revolutionary War was supplying information to King George's soldiers. The soldiers would then conduct foraging raids, stealing cows and food from area farmers.

Neighbors eventually found out about the Tory's actions and decided to take care of the scoundrel. A group of men dragged him up to the attic of Seven Stars, tied one end of a rope around his neck and the other around a wooden beam, and tossed him out the window.

In the 1930s there was a man living in the Salem area named John Klein. He was one of four harvesters employed to cut the grain for the Robbins family, who owned Seven Stars Tavern. Nathaniel ("Natty") Robbins always had difficulty in getting help locally because the house had a reputation for being haunted. Finally, Natty was fortunate enough to hire John Klein, who had no fear of ghosts, and three other itinerant workers, named Simon, Sam, and Jim.

It was the custom for farmhands to sleep in the large attic of the house, which was furnished only with some chairs, a bowl and pitcher on top of an old pine washstand, and straw mattresses on the floor. After their first day's work, the four men were too tired to notice the musty smell of old wood and moldy straw. All went to bed early that night, and their sleep was deep.

On the second day Simon went about his work with a glum silence that irritated his friends Jim and Sam. All four men worked hard and retired early that night, again from exhaustion; but before extinguishing the lamp, Simon asked if anyone had heard anything strange the night before. His friends at once connected this with his long face that day and assured him that he must have been dreaming. This is what he wanted to believe, but Simon was still uneasy, for he could not rid himself of the certainty that he had not been dreaming. His memory of the event was far too vivid.

Simon knew that if he said more, he would be ridiculed; as it was, his friends made jokes about his drinking too much of Natty's cider. The next day Simon's spirits were still melancholy. He avoided his friends entirely, and just before dark he made some pretext to slip away and climb up to the attic alone. When the others came up laughing and talking, they found Simon up in the rafters that supported the roof—marking crosses on the timbers with a

Seven Stars Tavern is said to be the champion haunted house of New Jersey.

piece of chalk. They joked about his "getting religion" so suddenly, but Simon said nothing, and as soon as he had swung himself down, he blew out his candle and turned in.

Something awakened Sam during the night, and to his astonishment he saw Simon seated on a chair, staring straight ahead and rigid as a post. At his feet were two lighted candles. The agony of fear on Simon's face was real.

"What's wrong?" asked Sam, springing to his feet.

"Shhh!" whispered Simon, holding up a hand to quiet him. His face was white and his eyes wide as he gazed in the direction of the stairway. Sam roused the two other men as quietly as possible, but perhaps he made more noise than he thought, for Simon repeatedly hissed "shhh" at them and motioned agitatedly for them to be quiet. The men could not help being frightened, although they had no idea what had happened. There was a terrifying sense of some imminent peril.

In profound silence they sat and waited. Finally, John Klein whispered, "What is it, Simon?"

"Shhh! Ghosts!" Simon whispered back. "I heard 'em again. They may come back up here. They're downstairs."

Klein was not afraid of ghosts, but Simon had shaken his confidence. It was not what Simon had said or even the conviction with which he had said it that upset Klein as much as the fact that, now and then, Simon would whisper a few stuttering words and then give a startled jump.

The story, as Klein was able to put it together, was that Simon had actually heard ghosts the night when the men said he had only been dreaming. At first, Simon said, the ghosts were far away. Then they came nearer. Finally, there had been a terrible scuffle on the stairway, with much shouting and swearing. A group of brawling spirits had come thronging up the ladder into the attic and headed for the window near Simon's mattress. "They pushed and shoved right up to my window and went out through it as if they were smoke! Twice now I've seen them and heard them."

"How do you know they're ghosts?" asked John Klein.

"If they were human, they would all be dead. That window is sixty feet above the ground, but they're not dead. I heard them clatter back in again. Shhh! They're downstairs now."

All was darkness except for the shadows of the men moving as the candles flickered. Simon made them lock the door at the foot of the stairway. Klein and Sam did so. Next Simon ordered that all the attic windows be closed and wedged, too, and they did that also. In silence they sat and waited, hearing only the beating of their own hearts. Simon would not let them set their chairs over any crack in the floor because, as he told them, "When the ghosts find the door barred, they'll come up through the cracks in the floor."

Not a sound. They were all apprehensive, yet there was nothing but a prolonged stillness. After some time had passed, Jim broke the silence and told the others they were all "blank fools" and that he was going back to bed. The rest followed sheepishly.

How long they had been asleep is uncertain, but they were brought to their feet by the most hellish screams of terror. Simon was nowhere to be seen. By the light of a candle that someone lit, they found him, almost hidden, down in the angle where the floor met the sloping roof, his face to the corner and his hands clasping his head. He was screaming and sobbing, praying and writhing, all the while kicking as if to get away from somebody or something.

Simon's screams brought up Natty Robbins and the women of the house. It was the women, more than the men, who finally succeeded in calming Simon down. This is the account he gave of what had happened after the four men had gone back to bed.

I was sound asleep. I didn't hear any noise at all, but, before God, when I woke up quick, I *felt* something. I tried not to do it, but I couldn't help pulling the sheet back and peeking out. There was nothing I could see, because the candles had been blown out, and there wasn't a bit of light. But I knew there was danger.

Suddenly, I heard a steady thump, thump, thump on the stairs, as if someone was striking with a light hammer, and my eyes were riveted in that direction. It was the pitch black of night, but just as plain as if he had been made of moonlight, I saw a man slowly coming up the stairs. First appeared his head, then his body, and finally his whole figure. He held the end of a heavy rope in his two hands. At each step, he hit the step ahead of him with the rope. Although he wore heavy boots, there was never a sound from them, only the thump, thump, thump of the rope end and a bubbling sound in his throat, as if he were trying to say something and couldn't.

After reaching the top of the stairs, he advanced straight toward the window by my bed. I thought that if I kept still and he didn't see me, he'd go on past me and out the window, as he had done on the previous night. Then I'd be well shut of him. But just before he got to my bed, he commenced a violent grabbing and tugging at his throat with his two hands. All the time he was making the most horrible choking noises and twisting his body and striking out with his boots in a way that I thought would be the end of me.

Then, all of a sudden, he quieted. He threw out his arms and raised his head as if praying, all the while moving toward the window. I had sense enough to know that he would soon be gone, and I felt easier. But when he was right opposite me, I could see that there was a rope tied tight around his neck and hanging down behind. God, how I remember the sound of that trailing rope, for I had heard it before, not knowing what it was.

My trouble had only begun, for instead of going on past me, as I had prayed he would, he suddenly halted, dropped his arms, and stood looking down at me. I tried to call the boys but was too terrified to make a sound.

Kneeling down, the ghost threw back his head and thrust his neck, with the rope around it, close before my face. I couldn't stir. He pointed to his throat, out of which were coming those ghastly gurgling noises, and he repeated those violent motions I had seen before. Now I saw that they were efforts to untie the rope. His face and neck were blue and swollen, and a bloody froth oozed from his lips.

He reached out and took my hands in his, raising them to his throat. I somehow found the strength to pull them back. He gently took them again, and something made me understand that he wanted me to loosen the knot. Somehow, I did it. I don't know how. He leaped up, uttering the most devilish "Ha! Ha! Ha!" and disappeared through the window. And that is the last I remember until daybreak.

Simon, Jim, and Sam left the tavern the next day. John Klein worked a day or two longer; then he, too left. Not that he was afraid of ghosts, he said, but because he couldn't get Simon's screams out of his ears. As he finished telling this story to his son, Klein shook his head and said, "What's the use of working all day at a place where you can't get any sleep at night?"

The Tory spy was never again seen at Seven Stars, and Klein swore that Simon's cries had scared him off, but others believe that Simon laid the ghost to rest when he was brave enough to untie the knot and free him.

———————

Said to be the best-preserved colonial tavern in the East, Seven Stars was built in 1762 by Peter and Elizabeth Lauterbach (later Louderback), whose descendants own the Louderback North American Van Lines. For more than a decade, the tavern was the home of Roy Plunkett, the inventor of Teflon. It is now the property of Robert Brooks of Woodstown. Though it is not open to the public, passersby may view it from the road at the intersection of Kings Highway and Woodstown–Auburn Road.

THE HOUSE OF SPIRITS

The Myrtles, St. Francisville, Louisiana

St. Francisville, Louisiana, is a charming old town some seventy miles north of New Orleans. It is built on a narrow ridge and said to be "two miles long and two yards wide." There are many beautiful plantation homes there, but the only one with eerie happenings that have reverberated throughout America is The Myrtles.

The Myrtles has been featured in *Life* magazine, *Southern Living*, *The Wall Street Journal*, *USA Today*, *Family Circle*, and many other publications. Many television networks have also done features on this house. The Myrtles is also, according to the U.S. Tourist Bureau, one of the authenticated haunted houses of America, and it has sometimes been called America's most haunted house.

The Myrtles contains some of the most interesting architecture in the South. The outside of the home, built by General David Bradford in 1796, has lacy, ornamental ironwork, and within, the large rooms, with their high ceilings, are graced by outstanding plaster friezes. It is surrounded by immense oak trees dripping with Spanish moss, and beneath their shade, the house appears to be in perpetual twilight. "Unlike other houses, to me, The Myrtles is an entity," says its owner, Frances Kermeen.

How did a vivacious blonde from the West Coast with hazel eyes, an attractive smile, and the voice of an engaging teenager become the owner of a house like this? And what eerie experiences has she encountered? Ms. Kermeen shares her story.

While I was on a cruise to Jamaica and Haiti and then on to Acapulco, I became friendly with a couple who talked me into skipping Acapulco and coming back to Louisiana with them. Because this is such a lovely place and, really, just for fun, I decided to look at real estate. The day I was looking was the day that the listing on The Myrtles came into the office.

I later found out that a couple who lived directly behind my parents' house in San Jose had gone on the same cruise I had (though twenty years earlier) and had stopped in St. Francisville on their way back to Michigan. The house happened to be for sale at the time, and they bought it under almost identical circumstances.

That first day in the real estate office, as we were going out to look at the house, the realtor kept calling me Sarah, although I corrected her several times. Neither of us were aware of it, but later I found that two Sarahs had lived here in the 1800s.

When I went into the place for the first time, I heard a woman's voice calling my name. At first I thought it was the realtor, but she was outside trying the back-door key to be sure that it worked. After I left, I knew I would be buying that house, and I cried some that night as I realized that from now on, I would be far from my family and home.

As I think about everything that happened, I feel that fate—I prefer to call it God—has played an important part in the events of my life. I also think that places exert a strong pull on certain individuals, and I will always believe that this house chose me.

The first week that I was there, I was sleeping in an upstairs bedroom. I left the lights on, but with the switch set on "dim." After a night or two, I thought that was silly and that I could sleep with the lights off, so I turned them off. But sometime after midnight I woke up, and the lights were on bright. Half asleep, I thought that I must have left them on, and I turned the dimmer. The room was once more in darkness. Two hours passed, and I was awake again. I found all the lights in the room on bright, just as they had been two hours earlier. I turned the switch 360 degrees and clicked the lights off again. Later I woke up for a third time, and the lights were on once more. That just scared me to death, and I grabbed my robe and blanket to go downstairs and sleep in the sitting room.

All went fine, and I slept peacefully until about five o'clock, when I woke up with a start and had the feeling that someone was looking at me. I stared up into the face of a large black lady whose head was wrapped in a green turban. She wore something that resembled a long, green dressing gown. I was so shocked that I just couldn't look at her face again. By that time I had begun screaming, but she still didn't go away. Involuntarily, I struck out with my arm to push her from me, but as I did so, my hand passed through her, and she faded away.

It was a couple of days before the closing on the house, and the current owner was still there. I told her about it the next day, and she said, "That's ridiculous!" But even on the first night, at about one o'clock, I had heard footsteps outside my door and assumed that it was one of the other houseguests. The next day I learned that everyone in the house claimed to have been dead to the world before eleven.

Later I found the whole town knew that the house was haunted, but they weren't going to tell an out-of-state person who was thinking about buying it. After I had bought the house, I mentioned the lady in green to the mother of the former owner, and to my surprise, she was absolutely thrilled. Can you imagine? She said, "Why, Frances, you have seen The Myrtles' most famous ghost!"

I turned the house into a bed-and-breakfast place, and at first I tried to keep the ghostly visitors a secret from the real ones. But during the seven years I have been here, there have been about a hundred reports each year of apparitions or some supernatural

Each room at The Myrtles has its own resident ghost.

occurrence. There were times when I was truly frightened, and the only thing that kept me from going back to my parents was that it would be too embarrassing to tell them that I was leaving because I was afraid of ghosts.

The most common sounds are either those of children's voices at play or that of a baby crying. But the eeriest of all is the music of a dance going on downstairs. Often people think that another guest's television is on too loud, but on inquiring they find there is no television set in the room next to them.

Each room has its own unique ghost. One has a wounded Confederate soldier who appears in May and June. A pair of honeymooners stayed here. The groom went upstairs alone to lie down and woke to find a black servant standing beside the bed bandaging his foot. The honeymooners immediately checked out.

The plantation's most famous murders occurred shortly after its sale in 1817 to a philandering judge named Clarke Woodruff, General Bradford's son-in-law. The judge grew angry with a slave woman named Cleo for eavesdropping, and he cut off one of her ears as a penalty. For revenge, she mixed poisonous oleander flowers into a birthday cake for the judge's oldest daughter. His two little girls died, as did his wife. Other slaves hanged Cleo. It is said that she still haunts the house, wearing a green turban to cover her missing ear. Cleo was evidently the ghost who frightened Frances Kermeen during her first week in the house.

Janet Roberts, a psychic who is the treasurer of the Louisiana Society for Psychical Phenomena, believes that The Myrtles has many ghosts. "Walking into the parlor was like walking into a crowded cocktail party. I felt that we were literally bumping into people, and I wanted to say, 'Excuse me.'" But except for the grumpy ghost who will occasionally hurl a clock or drop a candlestick, they do no harm.

Ms. Kermeen says, "At first I would not stay here alone at night. After I made it into a B&B in 1981, that seldom happened. But there are still a few things that rile me, and when they do, I have to go spend the night in the new wing."

Asked if she had ever talked with any of the apparitions, Ms. Kermeen shakes her head. "I certainly am not brave enough to try and communicate with any of them. I got used to the footsteps, the door slamming, and the voices, so now I don't keep my hand on the phone, ready to dial the police, as I did at first. I know this sounds absurd, but it's funny what you later come to accept when you didn't believe in this sort of thing at all before.

"About seventy-five percent of the people who come here do so because they want to hear about our ghosts. The other twenty-five percent just happen upon it. Oddly enough, the ones who get

scared and want to check out in the middle of the night are sometimes the big, macho-type men."

What sort of person is most apt to have a supernatural experience?
Says Ms. Kermeen, "It is usually the skeptic or the one who isn't
expecting anything to happen. When people have been so eager to see
a ghost and then report it, I wonder if it isn't their imagination."

She continues. "There have been ten murders here at The
Myrtles, and that's quite a few, even for a house that is almost two
hundred years old. I think some of those poor, tragic victims may
have been the ghosts I have seen. I believe that this house sets off
intense emotions in the people who live here for any length of time.
The overseer of this plantation in 1850 was a white man twenty-
four years old, and he committed suicide. I later hired a young man
of twenty-four who tried the same thing. Fortunately, he was
unsuccessful. He may have been unstable from the beginning, but
some people are very impressionable. I don't hire men that age anymore. I try to hire happy people, and I have always been a healthy,
happy person myself. Most visitors who come here seem to leave
content and rested. At least I think they do, for a great many return
each year.

"At first the ghosts terrified me. Then there was a year or two
when the knowledge that they were there was just fun and games.
But of late, I really believe that they have led me to God. They have
brought me closer to a sense of His reality and the meaning of life.
Once you are confronted with a ghost, you can't brush off the exis-
tence of life after death."

---

*For more information, write The Myrtles Plantation, Highway 61,
P.O. Box 387, St. Francisville, Louisiana 70775, or call (504)
635–6277.*

A PLEA FROM THE GRAVE

Cedarhurst Mansion, Huntsville, Alabama

There was food—champagne, caviar, paper-thin slices of Smithfield ham, canapes, smoked turkey, and more. A band played ragtime, jazz, the strident notes of "Somebody Stole My Gal," and then the romantic ballad "Roses Are Blooming in Tripoli," which started many of the guests reminiscing. The musicians played until shortly after midnight, and it was almost one o'clock before everyone had left.

Stephen Scott, of Germantown, Pennsylvania, along with several others, had been invited to Cedarhurst Mansion in Huntsville, Alabama, for the weekend. Stephen was enormously pleased when he saw Cedarhurst for the first time, for it was just the sort of home that he had always envisioned Southerners living in.

It wasn't quite as sumptuous as the houses in *Gone With the Wind*, Stephen thought as he dressed for the party, but it was still a magnificent place. He was amazed at the architecture—the rooms were immense, the ceilings high, the walls fifteen inches thick. That was why his room was pleasantly cool.

There was so much history here. In the early years families had lived close to each other, and the afternoon of the big party, Stephen had visited the family cemetery of the Ewings. Stephen S. Ewing had purchased land here in 1823 from Ebenezer Titus. (What an odd name Ebenezer was, Stephen mused. Were people ever named that anymore? It had some Biblical meaning, he thought.) Stephen had visited many of the Ewings that afternoon—not in the flesh, but at their graves. During the almost half a century that the family had lived in Cedarhurst Mansion, those who had passed on to the next world were buried out there in the cemetery.

Stephen rather enjoyed looking at the carved marble flowers and reading the inscriptions on the stones. Some of the epitaphs were admittedly flowery, but others had real feeling in them. These days a few words, or simply a name and date, suffice to characterize the deceased or the sentiments of those left behind. Were feelings deeper in the past, Stephen wondered, or were some of these epitaphs simply the custom of the period?

The next morning, he slept late. It was nine-thirty when he made his appearance at the breakfast table. His host and hostess were already having their coffee, and soon the cook appeared, carrying covered silver serving dishes from which rose the steam of scrambled eggs, grits, country ham, fried chicken, and hot biscuits. With the exception of the grits, which he considered tasteless, Stephen found everything delicious.

Stephen's life as a young stockbroker at a major Philadelphia firm was reasonably pleasant, and, even though his salary was a modest one, his parents had left him a comfortable income. Stephen had never been seriously interested in any woman and was quite content to return alone, night after night, to the family home. Nellie, the same lady who had helped his mother, still came each Monday and Thursday, as she had done for years. She would straighten the house, change the sheets, and see that "Mr. Stephen" had an ample supply of clean attire. On the first of October, Nellie put the down comforter on his bed; on the last day of March, she removed it and tucked in the lightweight summer blankets under the crocheted spread that his mother had made.

Back in his room at Cedarhurst Mansion that night, Stephen reflected on the day's events before going to bed. He liked people and fancied that he understood their feelings. Someday, when he retired, he thought he would write. The contribution he would make to literature would be stories about people he had known, stories filled with fresh, clever insights. He might even attempt a novel of manners mixed with humor, something that savored of Aldous Huxley. In any case, the novel would be pleasantly predictable, a tale with no violence and no disorderly, tragic lives with all their loose ends. The unpredictable gave Stephen indigestion, and he judged most people to be like himself: They simply didn't need another book to disturb them. Why couldn't more writers understand that?

He might start his writing career simply by doing an article now and then, perhaps a story about Cedarhurst. This was a delightful place, and such a story would give other Philadelphians an opportunity to experience vicariously a taste of what the Old South had really been like. He was sure that he could convey its gracious ambience in a manner that would arouse his friends' envy.

Stephen's thoughts were interrupted by the sound of distant thunder. The sheer white curtains at the open windows rippled as wind rushed through the trees. A summer shower was on the way, and that would cool things off nicely for tomorrow's activities with the other guests. Stephen fell asleep contentedly.

When he awoke, it was to the sight of one brilliant flash of lightning after another. Each sharp, explosive clap of accompanying thunder was followed by a succession of gradually receding rumbles. Stephen had been responsible for supplies at an ordnance department during World War II, and he recalled some explosives going off like that. The lightning and thunder continued, sounding uncomfortably close.

In his childhood, when he would visit his great-aunt and there was an electrical storm, the white-haired old lady and the little boy would retreat to her big bed for safety. Piling feather pillows all around them, she would hug him and reassure him that the pillows

Someone is in need of help at Cedarhurst mansion—but who?

would keep the lightning from striking. The curtains at Cedarhurst were now standing almost straight out, and gusts of rain had begun to pour through the windows onto the beautiful, wide-plank floors. Stephen thought of closing the curtains, but at that moment there came a crash of thunder so loud and so close that he felt it must surely have split the house asunder.

Sitting bolt upright in the big four-poster bed, he felt like dashing out into the hall to get away from the lightning. Instead, he closed his eyes and braced himself for the next detonation, but it did not come. It was passing over, he thought, and he opened his eyes.

Then he closed them tight, and next he blinked, but it did no good—for a girl in a long white dress was standing near the windows.

He buried his face in his pillow, and when he finally dared look again, the girl was gone. With a deep sigh of relief, Stephen pressed his arms close to his chest, hugged himself to keep from shaking, and started to lie down.

"Help me. Please, help me," came a feminine voice, and there she stood again, this time right beside his bed. Tall, with long, dark hair, she was very lovely, but Stephen was too shocked to appreciate her beauty.

"What kind of help?"

"This terrible wind has blown my tombstone over."

He was unable to reply.

"You aren't very gentlemanly."

"I'm sorry." He apologized, dimly aware that the wind had begun to blow again.

"You must come to the cemetery with me and set it up again."

Now Stephen knew what had happened. He had been struck by lightning and was dead. He was just as dead as the girl who was standing there speaking to him. He closed his eyes. When he opened them, she was gone. At that point he felt as if he were on a cloud drifting up in the air and through the sky—he didn't know where, and he didn't care.

The next morning was a glorious, sun-drenched day. Breakfast was served out on the side porch. It was nine o'clock, and everyone was there—with the exception of one guest, Stephen Scott.

"Shall we wait, or shall we eat without the sleepy sluggard?" joked one of the men.

"Let him sleep on. He was too popular with the ladies, anyway," laughed another.

"I think I'll go knock on Stephen's door," said their host.

At that moment the screen door to the porch opened, and everyone turned to look. It was Stephen, but his appearance was quite different from the night before. He was pale, and his hair and clothing were disheveled. Jokes about his late arrival evoked no answering smile.

"Did you rest well, Steve?" inquired his host.

"The storm woke me up."

"Quite something, wasn't it?"

"Ghastly, I'd say." Leaving his breakfast almost untouched, Stephen wiped his mouth with his napkin and rose from the table.

"Where are you off to, my friend?" asked his host.

"I want to walk out to the cemetery."

"At this time of morning? We were out there most of the afternoon yesterday, but if you want to go, I'll walk with you."

When they reached the cemetery, Stephen went directly to one grave. There, flat on the ground, lay the toppled tombstone of Miss Sally Carter, the sixteen-year-old sister of Mrs. Ewing. Miss Carter had died in 1837. He was certain now that it was Sally he had seen in his room.

Stephen's face grew pale. Pleading the sudden onset of illness, he terminated his visit to Cedarhurst well before nightfall.

It was odd, thought his host, that a man could be so shaken simply by a toppled stone on "Miss Sally's" grave.

In the early 1980s Cedarhurst, the historic Stephen Ewing house, and the land around it were sold. A developer has built private homes and town houses in the immediate vicinity. The restored house, at 2809 Whitesburg Drive in Huntsville, Alabama, now serves as a clubhouse for the Cedarhurst development. Its interior remains much the same. The cemetery was moved in 1983 to an undisclosed location. We wonder whether the move was as unsettling to Miss Sally Carter as a fallen tombstone was. Will she appear some night to another guest at Cedarhurst and tell him she needs his help?

THE HAUNTED HOTEL
Hotel Ione, Ione, California

At the foot of the Sierras in the California gold-rush country nestles the small village of Ione. On Ione's main street once stood an uncommonly haunted-looking hotel. The building was quintessential Old West. You almost expected a gunfight to erupt at any moment, shots to ring out, and a body to pitch headlong over the second-story balcony.

Millie and William Jones had longed to own this hotel for years; thus, when they were finally able to buy it, they could scarcely believe their good fortune. "We wanted to live here ourselves so that we could make it a hospitable place for other people. We moved into the three front rooms on the second floor," said Millie, but somehow her warmth and graciousness did not offset the atmosphere of the Hotel Ione.

When they bought the hotel in April of 1977, the Joneses were well aware that it needed extensive remodeling. So they began cleaning and painting. They even moved the dining room from the rear to its present position at the front, where we now sat with a view of Main Street. Millie told me the following story.

It was a warm afternoon, June 22nd, when I saw the first apparition. I was quite busy, for I was expecting the Chamber of Commerce for breakfast the next morning. Annie, our dishwasher, and I were the only ones there at that time of day. In the course of my preparations, I went back into the old dining room and was amazed at what I saw.

Floating in the air in the center of the room was a cloud of what appeared to be smoke. The strangest thing about it was that it did not dissipate but seemed to retain a pyramidal shape, except for a somewhat rounded top.

At first I was afraid that something must be on fire, but I checked and nothing had been left on the stove. For a little while I just stood there watching, almost hypnotized. Then I edged up closer and blew at it just as hard as I possibly could. I finally managed to blow it away. But in a minute or two, it came back again in exactly the same shape.

As I watched it hover there, it began to vibrate. And as that smoky form moved back and forth, I began to tremble and could feel every hair on the back of my neck stand straight up. I don't know when I have been so frightened. I knew I needed some help, so I hurried and got the dishwasher.

"Annie, there's smoke here in the dining room."

"There's nothing burning."

"I know, but what's that?" I asked, pointing at the pyramid.

"There's been a lot of people in here smoking."

"Not today. Not a living soul has been in here. It's not like smoke after people leave a room. I just blew this away, and it came back in the same shape."

"Don't tell me that! I was just in here and fanned it with this towel, and it went away and returned the same way," said Annie. And then she said, "I know what that is, but I don't want to say it, so we'll say it together."

"G-h-o-s-t," we both said, in shaky voices.

Then do you know what we did? We ran.

That was the first experience with our ghost, and, to the best of my knowledge, the spirit never came back in that form. During those first months that we were open, there was a customer who came to the hotel cafe regularly, a tall woman with piercing black eyes and straight, iron-gray hair that she wore in a large, soft bun at the back of her head. I remember her well.

She had studied life after death and the supernatural and religious aspects of the afterlife. A very serious, scholarly lady she was, with all sorts of degrees. Sometimes we talked a little about ghosts when she was here and I wasn't busy, and I made no bones about what a fright the shape in the old dining room had given Annie and me.

"I'll be glad to help you find out who it is," she offered.

"No, thanks," I said.

But she insisted on giving me her card just the same. "In the event you have any problems, I will be glad to come and help you."

Of course, my reaction was, what could a puff of smoke do?

As time went on, our dining room was completed. We had very nice flatwear and attractive placemats, and we put candles on each table. Let me tell you, there was a real thrill of accomplishment when we had it all ready for our first guests. There was just one problem, though, and it was so incredible that we didn't know what to do about it: Except for those at one table, the candles proceeded to light by themselves.

We tried leaving the dining room and locking the door after us, but when we came back in, the room was aglow with light. All the candles were burning. We managed to get most of them to stay out, but there was always one table where they would come back on, and that was the one right in the center of the room. This was the area where I had first seen the ghost.

Of course, it was vitally important that none of our guests see this strange phenomenon. One night we were expecting the prestigious Historical Society from Stanford University. Since they had made reservations for a dinner party, we were going to make sure all the candles did not relight by themselves: If any guests left early,

The Hotel Ione was said to be haunted by several apparitions.

we would not extinguish the candles at their tables. Moreover, we decided that after everyone was gone, we would simply remove all candles from the dining room. That should solve the problem.

But our troubles were not over. Shortly before our guests were to arrive, there was the most awful odor in the dining room, and I didn't know what in the world to do. Have you ever heard that spirits sometimes have an odor accompanying their presence?

Well, I rushed over to the hardware store, got a lamp with an aromatic candle in it, and proceeded to burn it in the dining room. In a few minutes the odor was completely gone, and I was so thankful, for everything smelled just wonderful. Everyone enjoyed a lovely dinner, and they lingered, drinking coffee and talking. Finally, after the last guest had left, after midnight, we removed the candlesticks and locked the door. The next morning I came down about five-thirty to fix breakfast, and the entire hotel smelled like frankincense and patchouli oil, sickeningly sweet.

When I unlocked the door to the back room, the candles were burning once more. They had been moved from the top shelf of my grandmother's buffet to the bottom shelf, and they were burned completely down to a tiny flame. That's when I called the lady who had offered to come if I needed help.

The hotel had burned down once, and by now you can understand that I was quite alarmed. I began to feel that this hotel was more subject to fire than most. We arranged for the woman who had studied the supernatural to come Saturday night at ten o'clock. I felt so silly even then that I remember joking, "It needs to be night, and I must have a black cat under the table."

When she arrived, I brought the whole staff into the dining room; then I thought it would be good if someone not connected with the hotel were present, too. I went to the front door, and the first person I found was a gentleman from here in town who was not intoxicated. I'm not saying that's unusual, but we were lucky, because it was Saturday night.

We all held hands and asked for a protective circle of faith from God, and each person said a prayer to himself for assistance in case this "thing" should come out. I had real reservations, and I said to the woman, "This could be frightening. It may be that I am exposing these people to something dangerous."

"They are here of their own free will," she said, and she began to talk to the darkness all around us. Beside her was a candle that she had blown out but which the apparition kept lighting. We had divided up some paper into several pieces, and we each had a pen.

"We know you are here, but who are you?" I heard her say.

Nothing happened, and all of us just rolled our eyes around, trying to see each other's face in the dark. I really was afraid, I must admit.

"Come on. You are disturbing Millie Jones, and I want to know who you are. You have a problem, and we can help you." There was no answer.

My heart began to thump so hard that that was all I could think about. Then came a startling noise. The medium had struck her hand sharply on the tabletop. I started to cry out and said, "I really don't want to do this." But I heard the harsh, almost angry voice of the medium speak to me.

"Hold on to your pen!"

My arm hurt between my elbow and hand and got very, very hot as the pen wrote. It was as if a strong but invisible hand were guiding my own. The words formed on the paper said "Mary Phelps." I read it and heard my own voice saying, "It fits myself," and the medium said, "All right, Mary Phelps, you have a problem. Now, how can we help you?" My hand began to move across the paper. I had to use my left hand to spread the pages out in order to hold the words.

Mary Phelps wrote that she lost a baby in a room fire in 1884. Other questions were asked, but no one got to write as I did. Someone asked what was the baby's name. The medium wrote "Baby Jon."

You just held your pen, though you did not have to hold on tightly. It just wrote, and when Mary Phelps was through talking through you, your arm relaxed. I tried to trick her; I asked what was the room number. They have been changed often, and sometimes on New Year's Eve one of the guests, as a prank, will change a room number.

I knew that the hotel had not burned until almost ten years later, in 1893, and I was puzzled. My hand began going back and forth and back and forth, and I thought it was just relaxing from having been used as an instrument. Around the whole table nothing was happening, except that my arm would not stop moving back and forth, until the medium said, "You must be more specific, Mary Phelps. Which room?"

At this question, the pen shot off the page in a sharp line, and then my arm went limp and dropped. I said, "I just can't imagine what this could be." Then I realized there were no room numbers then. In a moment my arm moved once more, and my hand, traveling across the page independent of my own will, wrote, "Go where the wall is bent."

Two days later a member of our bartending staff said, "Why, I know where the wall is bent. It's on the second floor, right outside Number 9." We assumed that this must have been the room in which the baby boy, Jon, died and that it was not a hotel fire, it was a room fire. That's why it was 1884 rather than 1893.

A year later, in October, I was cooking dinner. Eight people came in when we were almost ready to close. After they were served the waitress came back to the kitchen and said, "You have some fans in there who would like to meet the chef!" I went in and curtsied, and they applauded. A young lady in the party was especially enthusiastic.

"I just love this hotel. I don't know why we've never been here before, for we live in Calaveras County."

"That really isn't far from here. I hope you'll come again."

"Your waitress tells me you have ghosts?" came the unexpected reply.

"Yes, it seems to be a lady named Mary Phelps." When they heard that, the group went, "Oooh!" A Mexican gentleman among them turned to the young lady I had been talking with and said, "I'm going into the bar and talk with your husband. I don't want to hear this."

The face of the girl turned very white. "My maiden name was Mary Phelps. My grandmother and great-grandmother were named Mary Phelps, and at one time they lived in this old hotel!" You can be sure that I was as shocked as she.

The next day she came back, bringing her grandmother, who held in her hand a small, black, leather-covered diary written in Gaelic. She translated as she read from one of the pages written by a Mary Phelps in 1884. The words were, "I have recently lost my little son, Ian, in a hotel-room fire." In Gaelic, Ian means Jon. The entire family came back and burned a candle in the dining room for the child.

We heard no more from the spirit of Mary Phelps except on October 26 of 1980, just after we did a television show for "That's Incredible." At that time Mary Phelps was seen by a couple from Sacramento who, I think, were hoping to see another apparition who had been mentioned on the television show and who appears here occasionally. There was once a workman living here named George Williams; he would work quite late, and he didn't always bother to lock his room. When he returned, he would sometimes find that an intoxicated friend was asleep in his bed.

He would shake the bed until he could get the friend up, saying, "I'm sorry. You can't sleep here." George eventually died, but we have had complaints from men who have occupied his room. They say that an angry old fellow has pulled the covers off them and tried to shake them out of the bed, saying loudly, "I'm sorry. You can't sleep here!" I don't think he has ever bothered a woman in that room, only men.

The couple from Sacramento did not see George, but the wife had a vivid experience. She awakened to see a woman dressed in black with a little bonnet on and her arms stretched out, pleading with her.

"Help me get my baby out of the fire! Help me! Please, help

me!" said the woman. We were convinced that it was Mary Phelps. The couple had retired quickly after arriving the night before, and we had no opportunity to mention anything to them about Mary. The entire incident was remarkable. But finding out that Mary was a real person seems the strangest sort of coincidence, like something that would never happen in a million years," said Millie Jones, staring thoughtfully out at Main Street through the window of the hotel dining room.

"'Help me get my baby out,'" she said almost to herself, repeating Mary Phelps's plea. "The poor woman."

A year after this story was written, the Hotel Ione burned to the ground. The cause of the fire was never discovered. From its early years the hotel was subject to manifestations of fire, from the candles relighting to the mysterious smoky form that was sometimes seen floating through the air on the lower floor.

The Hotel Ione was at 41 Main Street, Ione, California. Should you ask me whether I think it was haunted or not, all I can say is that I felt it was from the moment I stood in the lobby and looked up the stairs to the second floor.

THE GHOST LOVER

The Alexander–Phillips House, Springfield, Massachusetts

It is doubtful whether the Society for the Preservation of New England Antiquities hosts many ghost-story programs. Even if it did, it seems unlikely that another story could be as unusual as this one. This story was first presented at a Society meeting by the son of Mrs. Julia Bowles (Alexander) Phillips twenty-five years after her death.

Fortunately, one of those present at that meeting was Richard C. Garvey, editor of the *Springfield Daily News.* His interest in history and his writing skills combine as he masterfully retells the following romantic and eerie story. Garvey's source was an account that Mrs. Phillips wrote in 1886 that was never made public until it was presented to the Society. He edited and paraphrased it for his newspaper. With his permission, the story below is reproduced as it appeared in the *Daily News.*

When my father bought Linden Hall, I was very young, only seven years old, but my first recollection of the house is quite distinct. I was first brought here by Father one afternoon when he came to talk over some business arrangement with the former owner, an elderly Southern lady who occupied it as a summer residence. She was accompanied by her family of two sons and a beautiful daughter, a retinue of slaves, and a fine yellow coach drawn by thoroughbred horses.

Soon we were established, and I and my young sister roamed at our own sweet will through the lofty rooms and the lovely gardens. The flower garden was the delight of my sister and myself. My sister was a strange child, fanciful and dreamy. Very soon I noticed that the house seemed to have a special charm for her. Our dining room was then in the eastern wing, the library in the western wing.

It is in this library wing that my story centers. We were still quite young when we learned that this library and the little bedroom opening out from it had been lived in for years by a young man, one of the sons of the Southern lady. During all this time, no one had looked upon his face. He was a very handsome fellow, they said, clever and fascinating in his manner, but like many attractive men with plenty of money, he had become dissipated and led a very fast life. Then, satiated with what he supposed to be the only pleasures of this world, he decided to isolate himself from his fellows and spend his remaining years in study and self-communion.

My sister, Leila, was a peculiar, reticent child, and this story naturally made a great impression upon her. In the summer, when the old library was opened, she spent a great deal of time there, sitting at the window that looked out upon the garden and reading the queer old books, especially those related to the supernatural. The years of our childhood rolled slowly by.

One warm Sunday afternoon early in June, when Leila was sixteen, she stood in the garden facing the library. She looked toward it, feeling drawn to do so by some strong impulse. There in the window sat a young man, and he seemed to her as beautiful as a god. His large, dark eyes rested upon her with a gaze of burning intensity.

She walked through the garden, around the pathway, and up the library porch steps, but on looking into the room, she was amazed to see the chair in the window empty! She came immediately back to the rest of the family and asked what young man had been in the library. We laughed and replied that she must have been dreaming.

This house was the scene of an exceptional courtship.

She turned away from us with a troubled look in her eyes.

She came to me one evening several days later and said, "I have seen him again." She told me that she had stepped out upon the eastern porch for a moment and was astonished to see, standing in the driveway, a spirited black horse saddled and bridled with rich, silver-mounted trappings. She turned her head and encountered again the face of the man she had seen at the library window.

Before she had time to speak or even think, he leaned toward her, grasped her hand on which he pressed a burning kiss, and, mounting his horse with a flying leap, galloped away in the dusk.

As Leila related this to me, she was trembling with intense excitement. She begged me to say nothing of the matter to our parents, and I consented, though greatly troubled.

It was about this time that Leila became a somnambulist. One night I was awakened from a heavy sleep by a slight noise. I lighted my bedside candle, hurried into my wrapper and slippers, and reached the foot of the stairs just as a white figure opened the library door and glided out onto the porch. I was not of a timid disposition, but the ghostlike apparition before me was almost too much for my nerves.

I recovered myself sufficiently to think that the figure looked like Leila. I hurried to her room. Both windows were open wide. The moonlight streamed in over the great fir tree, lighting up the whole chamber, and one hasty glance showed me that her bed was empty. I groped my way downstairs again and hurried out the library door.

Midway on the garden walk, I met Leila. She was walking slowly with wide-open eyes, utterly unconscious of my presence.

It struck me as very curious that she was completely dressed, in a soft white cashmere, her favorite dress, and her manner of walking was very peculiar. She seemed to be leaning toward someone. Her face was upturned with an expression of rapt attention, and now and then she smiled and moved her lips as if speaking, but I could distinguish neither words nor sound.

Without saying anything to Leila, I determined to speak to Mother, but I could not bring myself to mention the two strange meetings of which Leila had told me. To my surprise, Mother appeared to think little of the sleepwalking; she said that she herself had been subject to the affliction as a young girl. After that I became so accustomed to Leila's nocturnal walks in the garden that I am sure I slept through some of them.

The sultry days of August came. I had never known such oppressive heat. For weeks we had no rain. At last, one evening we started to bed feeling a slight breeze stirring, and we said hopefully, "Before morning, we shall have rain." I must have slept soundly for several hours before I was awakened by a frightful flash of lightning, followed immediately by a deafening crash. Before I could gather my senses, down came the longed-for rain, in drenching torrents.

My first thought was of the open windows throughout the house, and I flew from room to room closing them. On reaching Leila's room, a sudden flash illuminated the entire chamber and showed me that the room was empty.

"Leila is out in the storm!" I cried out, and two or three of us took a lantern and went into the garden. Halfway down the walk we found her—her life shattered by a lightning bolt!

We bore her into the house and up to her bed. It was then that we realized she was wearing Mother's wedding dress, from an old cedar chest in the garret. Leila had arrayed herself in the quaint, old-fashioned gown, and upon her head she had placed mother's bridal veil of antique lace.

The cruel lightning had failed to mar her exquisite beauty. Not until we had laid her away in the grave was everything explained. A few days after the funeral, I was in her room. On opening a little escritoire, I found a folded letter addressed to me in Leila's handwriting. The letter told me of the first time the handsome stranger in the garden spoke to her, and, when he did, it was a declaration of love!

This is what he told her:

"Leila, the power of love has drawn me from a far-off country to your side. Without question or fear, will you put your trust in me?" After quoting his words to her, she revealed her own plans, saying, "I am going to that far-off country from which he came to me, and it may be many years before I shall see you all again."

It was her goodbye. This astonishing confession of Leila's was never known before outside the family.

Years went by and the city grew. Finally, through the constant raising of the street, the house seemed so low that Father thought it advisable to move it to the side lawn where it now stands. When the library wing was removed, the workmen discovered in the low cellar beneath the bedroom the skeleton of a man. It was given decent burial near the graves of our own dead, and Father yielded to what he thought was a peculiar fancy of mine: He buried the man's bones beside Leila's.

———————————

The Alexander-Phillips House, one of Springfield's most famous residences, was built in 1816 according to the design of Asher Benjamin, then America's leading architect. It is closed to the public, but its exterior may be viewed at 289 State Street, between Elliot and Spring Streets in Springfield, Massachusetts.

A DRUM FOR THE DEAD

Berkeley Hundred, Charles City, Virginia

When I first saw him, the master of Berkeley was out picking up limbs that the wind's hands had stripped from ancient oaks. With his eighty-two years, Malcolm Jamieson stood like one of the oaks, aged but sturdy. Beneath his shock of white hair, the blue wells of his eyes gazed out with humor and kindness.

No Virginian he, but from energetic Yankee stock, Malcolm Jamieson, through both physical labor and imagination, wrested this gem of an early colonial plantation from the years of neglect following the Civil War.

In a very real sense, Berkeley is the home of all Americans, for it is the birthplace of a signer of the Declaration of Independence and the ancestral home of two presidents. Over the past three-and-a-half centuries, this single plantation has seen more historic firsts than any other English-speaking settlement in America.

By the spring of 1622, just as the Virginia settlement was gaining strength, the inhabitants of Berkeley met with sudden and violent death during an Indian uprising. The Indians simultaneously invaded plantations all over the colony, seeking to annihilate the English intruders. At Berkeley they succeeded; the original plantation never fully recovered from the massacre although it changed hands several times during the next seventy years.

The Harrison family acquired Berkeley in 1691. The history of this family and American politics blend together here like the sweeping green lawn and fields running down to the banks of the James River. One descendant, Benjamin Harrison V, grew up to sign the Declaration of Independence. His good friend George Washington was often entertained at Berkeley. In fact, every one of America's first ten presidents enjoyed the plantation's hospitality. Two of these presidents came from the Harrison family—one was William Henry and the other, his grandson.

By the nineteenth century financial reverses had caused the Harrison family to lose its hold on Berkeley, and then Virginia was torn by the Civil War. General McClellan's Federal troops occupied Berkeley after retreating from their siege of Richmond. On the grounds and fields surrounding this once proud manor house, the Union Army of the Potomac encamped, 140,000 strong, receiving supplies from U.S. Navy gunboats anchored in the Potomac River.

During that hot August of 1864 at Berkeley, a man named General Daniel Butterfield composed a haunting bugle melody. The name of it was "Taps." It was a melody that would soon drift out through the darkness into camps all over the world.

As Jamieson walked about picking up limbs on a warm autumn day in 1987, he thought about Berkeley's history. A panorama of scenes went through his mind leading from the past to the present, peopled by characters whom in a sense he felt he had come to know intimately.

It was on that day in 1987 that a white Oldsmobile station wagon rolled up to Berkeley and a family from Richmond, whom we shall call the Larrimores, began the plantation tour. Julie Larrimore was more patient than her brother. Randy, not content to inspect all the fine architectural details of the mansion and eager to explore the farthest reaches of the plantation, slipped away during the movie about the plantation's history.

Randy always became restless when he had to tag along with his parents on tours of old houses, for he would rather be out tramping

Berkeley Plantation is on Highway 5 in Charles City, Virginia.

in the woods, slogging along in the muck beside a river, or peering curiously into the musty dimness of an old barn. In the darkness of the visitor center where tourists were viewing the film, he had seized his chance to slip away. Perhaps, he could even melt back into the group as they came outside later. Meanwhile he was off in search of adventure.

"This house was purchased by John Jamieson of Scotland, who served as a drummer boy in McClellan's army fifty years ago," intoned the film's narrator. "In 1927 the plantation was inherited by his son, Malcolm, and together with his wife, Grace, they are responsible for the extensive restoration seen today.

"Window frames, floors, and masonry as well as America's finest pediment roof, are all original. Much of the furniture came from Westover Plantation, and the English silver, Waterford glass, and Chinese porcelain are authentic to the period. The famous Adams woodwork was installed in 1790. Berkeley's five terraces between the house and the James River were dug by hand, using oxcarts and wheelbarrows, before the Revolution."

Outdoors, Randy had already reached the third terrace and was contemplating which part of the plantation he wanted to explore first. His parents continued to watch the film, unaware that he was no longer with them. "Today, the soybean and small grain crops that occupy more than a thousand acres of this working plantation are harvested with the latest in farm equipment. So, welcome home, Americans, to a plantation where history lives today. We hope you enjoy your visit," said the narrator.

Julie and her parents filed out with the rest of the audience. She was just about to tell them that Randy was gone when they saw friends. Everyone began talking and when Julie found that their daughter of her age was with them, she forgot all about Randy's defection. While they had been in the house, there had been a summer storm; the sky had become quite dark, though it was not yet midday.

Randy had decided in favor of the riverbank. He, as usual, had forgotten the time, and he paid no attention to the darkening sky or even the first drops of rain. Over his head, thunder crashed like colliding freight cars, and flashes of lightning were all around him.

He was not easily frightened, but he couldn't help but think of the story of how, long ago, Benjamin Harrison and his son had been lowering one of the windows upstairs, when the boy was struck and killed by lightning. Mr. Jamieson had said that often when he was relating the story of the boy being killed at the window, a noisy crash would be heard, and everyone would hurry upstairs to discover that the open window had slammed closed.

Then Randy saw a red-headed boy a few yards away beckoning to him. In a moment the pair stood together in a sheltered place where no rain was falling.

"This is a real cloudburst," said the boy.

"It's the lightning that bothers me," admitted Randy.

"I'll bet you're thinking about that story of Mr. Harrison's son being killed at the window."

"I guess I was."

"I used to think about it, too, when we were here and a bad storm would wake me up at night. A tent never seemed like much protection."

"You've camped out here beside the river?"

"Yes, many a night. My name is John. What is yours?

"I'm Randy. Say, you've got a nice drum there. Did it take you long to learn to play it?"

"No. You can't tune it, but I like the rhythm. Reminds me of my father when he used to play the bagpipes. Of course, they carry a tune, but there is a rhythm about their music, and drums have it, too."

"I wish my father could play the bagpipes. Do you come out here to camp often?"

"The camping? Oh, that was a long time ago." By now the rain had stopped.

"I could come and camp sometime, maybe, if I asked my dad."

And that reminded Randy that he had better get back to the house quickly. He turned to say goodbye to his drummer friend, but the red-headed boy was gone. He would get his father and together they would find him.

An excited Randy appeared just as his family was almost ready to go into the little restaurant that Berkeley maintains for visitors.

"Dad, I want you to come and meet my new friend!"

His parents were taking some pictures of the front of the house and Randy tugged at his father's arm to get his attention.

"Oh, all right," said his dad. "Where is this boy?"

"Near the river."

"Your mother would like to have lunch while we are here, but she can probably look around in the gift shop for a few minutes. Let's go find him."

The pair took a path that led off toward the left, Randy chattering away.

"Dad, he was wearing a uniform and carrying a drum."

"Some of the people around here are dressed in costume, I suppose."

"He must be hot in that uniform."

"He's probably used to it." They searched until his father was impatient to go to the restaurant, but they could not find Randy's new friend.

When dusk falls across the emerald fields of Berkeley and the last tourist has left, Berkeley's *real* inhabitants return. Although Randy did not know it, among McClellan's troops there was a lad born in Scotland, not old enough to fight in a war, but spunky enough to want to go. This brave twelve-year-old became a drummer boy, practicing until the alternate double strokes of the sticks upon his field drum produced a rhythmic, stirring call to battle. Its rumble could be heard through the trees like distant thunder.

Randy is not the only one to have seen him. Some say that the boy stands on the gently sloping hill several hundred yards above the James River near the Old Cemetery and by the split-rail fence, a red-headed youth striking his drum softly and gazing out over the river. Others relate having seen the figure of a uniformed youth with a drum strolling beside the riverbank and then back in the direction of the cemetery.

It may be that the young ghost drummer, still sometimes seen at

Berkeley, is the father of Malcolm Jamieson, the current owner. For it was John Jamieson who returned years later and bought the plantation where he was once a drummer boy with McClellan's army.

Do rooms in old houses harbor sounds of past events, latent, ready to be touched off by some slight vibration, rare frequency, or even an echo? Now and then in the afterdusk, faint laughter, tinkling glasses, and the murmur of voices have been heard. Could it be one of the many genial gatherings that the rooms of this home have seen?

There have been other reports of unusual sightings at this meeting-place of historic events and people, such as a tall, gaunt figure, down at the water's edge, walking slowly toward Berkeley. Abraham Lincoln himself had been to Berkeley twice during the war. Does he return to review his army? On the way the figure is sometimes accompanied by a little drummer boy, and together they turn right up the path, toward the hill with the split-rail fence. The two are obviously friends. Does the drummer boy remind President Lincoln of his own son?

If you are among the very fortunate, you might behold two shadowy figures cresting the hill some September evening or hear the last faint roll of a drum as they disappear from view. And while a late summer storm rumbles overhead, what is that on the far side of the rise? Can it be the Army of the Potomac, passing in review for Lincoln?

Berkeley Plantation is on Highway 5 in Charles City, Virginia. It is open year-round. To check visiting hours, call (904) 829-6018. The restaurant on the grounds serves a delicious lunch, replete with Southern specialties.

THE ROMANTIC INN BY THE SEA

Inn by the Sea, Cape Elizabeth, Maine

He needed to get away from the pace of speaking engagements, even from his much-loved research. Four days at the luxurious Inn by the Sea in Maine was to be his lesson in relaxation. He had just flown in from Chicago and was sitting in his armchair at home when Lydia handed him a copy of *The Discerning Traveler.*

"Look, honey. They describe this inn as "a romantic hideaway,"" she said, with a warm, inviting smile.

"I'm ready for that," said Mark.

Driving out of Boston on a Thursday in July, Professor Mark Hardee found himself looking forward to the experience. By afternoon he was driving his black Cherokee out on Cape Elizabeth along the Bowery Beach Road eagerly anticipating his wife's arrival. Lydia would be joining him in a few hours. He wished that she had not had to give a test at summer school this afternoon so that they could have driven up together.

"We work too hard. We must take the time to store up more good memories," she had said.

She had read about the Cape and described its picturesque old buildings with her usual boundless enthusiasm. He saw several thriving family farms, spotted two state parks on the Cape, and noticed with amusement that the town had taken a former fort and turned it into a recreation area. Mark also liked Cape Elizabeth's red-roofed houses, the lighthouse, and the nearness of the water. Looking around him, he saw much that was typical of New England.

His first glimpse of the Inn by the Sea came as something of a shock. Lydia had given him no idea of its size. It was an immense, gray-shingled complex, bordering Crescent Beach State Park. Strolling into the marble-tiled lobby, he was surprised to see the walls decorated with original oversize Audubon prints of coastal birds. A biology professor and occasional birder, Mark's spirits soared. He knew already that he was going to love this place.

Lydia had reserved a very luxurious suite. It had contemporary furnishings, a living room with a window wall, a two-story cathedral ceiling, and an oversize bath with a deep soaking tub big enough for two. Picking up one of the brochures on the bedside table, Mark saw a picture of an outdoor pool, a tennis court, bicycles, and a boardwalk that he presumed led to the beach beyond the park. He lay down on the sofa to read it and before long was obeying Lydia's admonition to relax: He was soon fast asleep.

When he woke up, someone was kissing him.

"I'm here, Sleeping Beauty," said his wife.

They had a late dinner on the porch of the dining room, selecting a table with a view. Champagne and appetizers of grilled shrimp served with fig and date chutney preceded a tender duck entree.

"Not at all bad for two teachers," said Mark. "I like this place. You are a woman of taste."

"Aunt Margaret would have approved," said Lydia, whose aunt had left her a small inheritance.

The next morning they went bicycling down Route 77 to the Portland Head Lighthouse, took the usual tourist pictures, and lunched at the Lobster Shack. Then they returned to the inn, pleasantly tired. On Saturday they cycled south to see Winslow Homer's studio at Prouts Neck.

They saved Sunday, the third day of their long weekend, for a lazy afternoon and evening out on the beach. Carrying a hamper with a picnic supper, Mark and Lydia ambled along the boardwalk leading from the inn. When they emerged from the state park, they found not a rock-lined shore but a magnificent sand beach stretching for miles beside the Atlantic. Mark wandered along near the water watching for unusual shells and sea creatures. Lydia read a book on the area.

She was a history teacher, and it amused him to hear her say things like, "I wish I could have lived back then," or "Wouldn't it be exciting to go through an experience like that?"

"You mean like the French Revolution or the San Francisco fire?" he would sometimes counter teasingly.

"Well, what have you learned about Cape Elizabeth?" he asked now, sitting down on the sand.

"I've found out that the Jordans were a very prominent family here."

"I'm sure they were, if they were your ancestors," quipped Mark. Before their marriage, his wife had been Lydia Jordan.

"I have no idea whether these particular Jordans were my ancestors or not, only that they were here in the 1630s and lived through three wars—the war of King Philip of Spain, King William's War, and Queen Anne's."

"They certainly suffered a long streak of misfortune," said Mark. "But you sound as if it had just happened."

"You aren't very sympathetic. I feel sorry for them," she said indignantly. "Just imagine. They had to leave during every war. Then, when they did come back in 1715, they were attacked by pirates."

"I'm glad they survived it, especially if they were your ancestors; it wouldn't surprise me if some of them were pirates. They settled all along the coast." Lydia made a wry face at him.

"Do you think Blackbeard ever got up beyond Philadelphia and New York?" Mark asked.

A nineteenth-century shipwreck ocurred offshore from where the Inn by the Sea now stands.

"Of course he did. They say he caroused with his pirate friends at Newport and buried treasure on an island off the New England coast. If you didn't work all the time, we could go searching for it."

"A biologist would rather search for rare bugs, my dear, but tell me more."

"Fishing was big here in the 1800s. During the winter men sailed to the Caribbean islands with cargoes of fish and lumber and brought back sugar and rum. But the part that interested me most . . ."

"Yes?"

"It was the number of shipwrecks off this Cape. I began to wonder why people settled here. There were bad storms, and over there near Richmond Island," she pointed, "is a ridge of rocks, under the surface of the water near shore. It's called Watts Ledge. I can just visualize fog and ships heading for Portland Harbor, getting off course and wrecking on it. Can't you?"

"I suppose so."

"Sometimes I think you're not very imaginative," she said reproachfully.

"Maybe not, but isn't one of us in the family enough?" He grinned at Lydia.

Unfortunately, the day that they had selected to spend out on the beach was cooler than anticipated.

"It's darned chilly out here without jackets, honey. Let's talk about all this back in the room. Better yet, we could go into the dining room and settle the seafaring history of Cape Elizabeth over a cup of hot coffee and dessert."

Mark was beginning to unwind, and he knew that he had been working too hard. There never seemed to be any time left over for themselves. They went to bed about ten o'clock, but he was unable to sleep. He always liked to walk while he thought about problems, and he was tempted to do so now, but where? At eleven o'clock he got out of bed, pulled on a pair of chinos, a shirt, and his hooded red anorak. On an impulse, he decided to go down to the ocean.

"What are you doing?" murmured Lydia sleepily.

"Dressing. I just want to walk for a while."

"Want me to come, too?"

"I won't be long. Why don't you go back to sleep?"

She closed her eyes.

The noise of the surf drowned out the sound of his footsteps on the boardwalk. A heavy sea was running, and fog swirled over the dark, turbulent water. He felt its mist on his face. Mark was not much happier walking than he had been in bed trying to sleep. What time was it? Almost midnight, he thought. Lydia would be worried if he was gone too long. It was while he was trying to wipe off his glasses and check the luminous dial of his watch that he heard it: A sharp crack, followed by the noisy wrench of shattering spars and timbers. For a few seconds there was complete silence.

Then the night was rent by a woman's screams. They came from across the water, but not far from shore. Loud shrieks floated toward him—those of women and children, their voices full of terror, and the hoarse shouts of men. Mark strained his eyes staring out to sea. He thought that he could pick out a dark mass silhouetted dimly between billows of mist. His heart was pounding. A ship had struck Watt's Ledge! It was in the direction of Richmond Island, and the calls for help were terrible to hear.

Mark raced across the sand to summon help. As he ran, he heard one last piercing cry from the direction of the water—the voice of a young woman. When he reached the boardwalk he almost collided with a shadowy, hooded figure.

"We've got to get help!" he shouted breathlessly to whoever it was. But the figure moved to block his way. He tried to push past when suddenly a beam of a light almost blinded him.

"Mark! It's me."

Lydia was standing with a raincoat over her gown, shining a flashlight in his face. "What's the matter?"

He caught her arm. "We've got to hurry. There's a wrecked ship close to shore!"

"How do you know?"

"My God! Can't you hear the screams?" he bellowed at her. "People are drowning out there!"

"I don't hear any screams. Just the roar of the surf."

The chorus of cries was ringing in his ears.

"Mark, stand still for a minute. You're trembling."

The cries were fainter and farther away now. Why couldn't Lydia hear them?

"I can't imagine what's happened to you. It has to be overwork," she said soothingly as she put her arm through Mark's.

Perhaps she was right, he thought. They walked back to the inn.

"Your nerves are strung tight—too many deadlines." She helped him off with his clothes. "Can you sleep now?"

"I think so," and he did. He was utterly exhausted.

The next morning Lydia tactfully avoided mentioning the incident of the night before. They breakfasted on eggs Benedict with fresh lobster meat, and afterward, to her surprise, Mark suggested stopping by the library.

"I just want to see their clipping file on shipwrecks," he explained.

"So now you're the one who wants to go to libraries and look up history," said Lydia, as they entered Thomas Memorial Library. Mark opened a manila folder and began searching through a huge pile of clippings.

"I think I've found it," said Mark. "Here's a story from March 1965 on shipwrecks of Casco Bay." The story was headlined, "*Schooner Charles* Crashed on Watt's Ledge in 1807."

"Look at this. The date the ship wrecked was Sunday night, July 12. It was a little before midnight when she hit the ledge and began to break up. Sixteen passengers drowned. It couldn't have been far from the beach. Three were able to swim to shore. "

"Have you seen the grave of the young woman who was coming back on the *Charles* from Boston? She was buying her trousseau," said the librarian. "Her gravestone is right near Crescent Beach. You should look at it before you leave Inn by the Sea."

"You know, there has always been a romantic story about that wreck," volunteered an old man who stood listening with open curiosity. "In the years since it happened, people walking on the beach at night have sometimes reported hearing the sounds of a shipwreck and the terrible screams of drowning passengers. The schooner was in so close that villagers at Cape Elizabeth heard the cries for help, and it made a deep impression upon them. Remarkable story isn't it?"

"Yes, it is." said Mark, a peculiar look on his face. This did not fit in with any of his experience as a biology professor.

He and Lydia found the gray slate marker at the girl's grave not far from the inn. It read in part: "Sacred to the memory of Miss Lydia Carver, age 24; who with 15 other unfortunate passengers perished in the merciless waves, by the shipwreck of the *Schooner Charles* . . . on Sunday night, July 12, 1807.

"Yesterday was July 12th," said Mark thoughtfully, "and Sunday night."

But Lydia hadn't heard. She gazed at the marker as if hypnotized. "Mark, do you notice how similar her name and mine are? They are almost the same! I was a Lydia Carver, too, except that my name was Lydia Carver Jordan. I even bought my trousseau in Boston, just like she did." Lydia's face was pale, and her eyes had filled with tears. "Poor girl," she said.

"You're right! What a coincidence. I think she may have become a romantic figure after the wreck, and perhaps, you were a namesake of hers." He remembered the frightened screams of the women he had heard the night before and thought about the bereaved fiancee.

He shivered as they stood there in the hot sun looking at the girl's grave. Could something have drawn his own Lydia here on this date?

The past would never seem as remote to him again.

––––––––––––––––

The Inn by the Sea is at 40 Bowery Beach Road, Cape Elizabeth, Maine. For more information, call (207) 799–3134.

WHERE YOU NEVER DINE ALONE

John Stone's Inn, Ashland Massachusetts

As Dwayne and Rita Doughtry left their apartment on the out-skirts of Boston to go out to dinner, Rita was still urging her husband to change his mind and go to a restaurant nearby.

"Ashland is twenty-five miles from here," she complained, "and the weather report says it may snow tonight."

"There's always that possibility in winter," said Dwayne, "but we can't hibernate until spring."

His wife looked at him crossly. "But I hate driving in snow."

"That's because you're from the South and not used to it."

"No. It's not that. I don't know why I feel this way tonight. It's like something is going to happen, and part of it will be because of snow, that's all."

"Something *will* happen. We will eat a sumptuous dinner in a historic inn where the past will come alive."

About forty minutes later the Doughtrys were entering Ashland, driving toward the center of town. They heard the mournful wail of a train whistle. Then came the noisy clatter of the wheels as a diesel engine, car after car rumbling behind it, sped by. The track was very close to the road. Wham, wham, wham, went the freight cars as they passed. Rita sat quietly, watching the slots of gray March dusk pass swiftly between each car and giving herself up to the hypnotic sight. She could feel the nose of their Honda shuddering at the impact of the wind from the train.

"It runs right through the middle of town, just the way trains used to do," said Dwayne nostalgically. "Doesn't slow much for Ashland, does it."

"No. It certainly doesn't." Trains weren't one of Rita's favorite topics. She'd had a "conflict of interest" with one once about a crossing, and the train had won. Rita had miraculously emerged unscathed, but the incident had made her heart beat faster every time she saw a crossbars without a gate and heard the approach of a train.

"The inn should be right along here somewhere."

She turned and saw it. "There it is on the corner. Oh, Dwayne. I love it!" They parked and got out of the car.

John Stone's Inn, at 179 Main Street, was painted a cheery New England red, and for a moment Rita stood staring at it and the black colonial-style sign out in front. On it was painted the stern countenance of a man of another era. An old-fashioned balcony on the second floor was supported by white columns running the length of the inn. On the third floor, two dormer windows perched near the peak of the roof.

Lights glowed welcomingly in the windows of the first two floors and the large wing on the side. Only the windows on the third floor were dark.

"It would look perfect on a Christmas card, if only those gables were lighted, too," said Rita.

"Yes, it would," said Dwayne. "Let's go in. I'm freezing!"

Once seated in the restaurant, Rita took off the hunter-green car coat with its hood. Holding the menu in one hand, she fluffed out the back of her long black hair with the other. How lovely she was, thought Dwayne, watching her as she studied the menu. She debated between beef Bourguignon and chicken Gran Marnier.

"Two brandies first, please," said Dwayne to the waiter, after

The manager at John Stone's Inn always looked after his guests—and maybe still does.

they had both decided on the beef. They carried their glasses over to the fireplace, and Rita talked about an upcoming magazine story, a trip trailing tigers in Sumatra. She was a freelance writer. How could she be so daring about some things and so fearful about others, he wondered.

"Old John Stone is giving us the eye," said Dwayne. "See his picture over the bar?"

Rita turned her head and smiled. "He almost seems to know something we don't. A secret?"

At that moment the front door opened, and an icy gust blew in with two couples, their coats flecked with snow.

"A real blizzard's blowing up out there!" said one of the women shivering."

"Not much chance of that this time of year, ma'am," replied the hostess.

Dwayne saw Rita pale, but she turned away from the new arrivals. She was listening to one of the boys clearing a table. "But sir, I did see someone downstairs near the storage room," he was saying to the manager. The rest was lost, for the boy was hustled into the kitchen.

"It's a good time for the grand tour of the inn while everyone is waiting for their food. Would you like to go along?" asked the hostess, stopping by the fireplace.

"That sounds wonderful!" said Rita.

"Well, if it's no trouble," Dwayne replied, with limited enthusiasm; he was enjoying the warmth of the fire.

Joining them, the young assistant manager had overheard the exchange. "Oh, no. My pleasure," he replied. Several other diners came, too, and they all formed a procession down the stairs into the cellar.

"Slaves were kept here in this hidden room during the Civil War until it was safe for them to go on their way to Canada," their guide said, with the air of one who had given this tour many times before. "It was part of the Underground Railroad," he explained. "I've heard stories that some people have heard the voices of the slaves singing. Then there is a story about the ghost of a little girl. People who have seen her say that she sits staring forlornly through the kitchen window."

"Oh, I hope we will see something tonight!" giggled one of the women.

"Well, I can't guarantee that, but we have had all sorts of odd phenomena. Glasses floating through the air, an ashtray suddenly splitting in two . . . once a tray flew through the air and hit one of us in the head."

"O-o-o-h. Watch out guys!" said the same woman. "You'd probably be the very one something would happen to, Joe," she said, grasping her husband's arm.

"Down here is where something *really* scary happened," continued their guide. "A manager who once worked here was in this room and saw a transparent figure that he was convinced was old man John Stone. Bad thing about it was, he saw it just before his own death. All the help thought it had been a sign, a kind of warning." He opened another door. "This used to be a game room. Stone and his friends were playing poker one night and one of the players, a salesman, accused them of cheating.

"Old John was enraged," continued their guide, warming to his story. "Swinging his clenched fist"—the assistant manager showed them how—"Stone, with one blow to the head, struck the salesman and killed him. I've always heard that his body is buried somewhere beneath this floor."

Rita shivered. The other guests looked like they wished something would happen, but no spirits put in an appearance, nor did anything else out of the ordinary occur. The tour was drawing to a close.

"One word of warning," said the assistant manager with a grin. "Remember that when you dine at John Stone's Inn, you never dine alone. At least that's what people here in Ashland say." There was a momentary silence. Then someone laughed, and the others joined in.

"I propose a toast to an unforgettable evening," said Dwayne, back at their table. He raised his brandy glass, waiting for Rita to follow suit, but she hesitated.

Her lips parted in an amused smile. "Does 'unforgettable' mean I'll see a ghost, honey? If it does, I'll drink to that."

As the brandy touched Dwayne's lips, the oddest thing happened: He felt a firm tap on his left shoulder. "Yes?" he said turning his head. No one was there.

"What did you say, honey?" said Rita, looking up.

"Nothing. Just thinking out loud," Dwayne improvised quickly. He must have imagined that someone had touched his shoulder.

That's all it could have been, but it left him with an uneasy feeling that was not to go away.

The Doughtrys ate in silence. They heard the long, drawn-out whistle of one of the many passing trains, then the sound of the locomotive and the rumble of the cars as they went by.

"A train whistle has an eerie sound at night, doesn't it?" said Rita.

"Oh, I don't know," said her husband. It did, though, and for some reason Dwayne was beginning to feel the faintest sense of dread. Had it started with Rita's original desire to go somewhere else? Or was it the tap that he thought he had felt on his shoulder? He dismissed these things as foolishness.

Dwayne glanced at his wife and saw her wince slightly and move her hand. "What's the matter?" he asked sharply.

"Nothing. For a moment I thought I felt something touch me."

"Like what?"

"A little like . . . well . . . like fingers placed over my hand," she stammered, flushing with embarrassment at how melodramatic her words sounded.

"That's ridiculous!" Dwayne said, a little too loudly. He knew he was overreacting and went on lamely. "Perhaps someone touched you accidentally as they passed our table?"

"I'm sure that was it," agreed Rita. "Did you know that this inn was built more than a hundred and fifty years ago?" she said, changing the subject.

"Yes. I read it on the back of the menu."

"It was finished in 1833 by a wealthy sea captain named John Stone. The inn is named after him."

"Figures," said Dwayne smiling.

Rita gazed with interest up at the exposed beams. "I know a magazine that runs pieces on early American homes and inns. It would probably buy a story on this place."

"Snow's stopped," announced a new arrival.

Dwayne saw Rita's shoulders relax, and she leaned back more comfortably in her chair. There was something about her now that reminded him of a lovely, sleek cat lolling in a comfortable spot. He guessed that she had been uptight about the weather and that that had started her imagination working overtime. Fingers touching her hand, indeed.

But he, too, was relieved that the snow had stopped. So why couldn't he rid himself of this crazy sense of dread? If there were really ghosts here, what dire meaning could a tap on the shoulder have? Was it to warn him that *his* time had come? Even thinking something like that really made him a first-class crazy, thought Dwayne. He sipped the last of his coffee.

Helping Rita on with her coat, Dwayne gave her a little hug. The evening had been pleasant. But he had the feeling that it was not over . . . at least not yet. At the cash register he thanked the assistant manager for the tour.

Dwayne opened the door of John Stone's Inn and emerged to find that snow was falling again—heavily. Within seconds he could hardly see Rita. She was halfway across the street when he caught up with her hurrying figure. This was almost a blizzard. Could he see well enough to drive back to Boston in weather like this? They heard the sound of a train whistle.

Suddenly, Dwayne squeezed Rita's arm. "Look! There's a stalled car on the track and a man trying to push it off. My God! A train's coming!"

Even with the flakes swirling around them, they saw the snow-covered figure on the tracks pushing the rear of a sedan. A woman screamed. Again they heard the wail of the whistle. Dwayne dashed toward the stalled car, Rita following. They heard the roar of the fast-approaching train.

"Stop! Dwayne—stop!" Rita shouted, but her husband never

heard her. Her cry was lost in the clatter of train wheels. The engine burst out of the darkness, striking the car with a horrendous crash. Rita heard the tearing of metal and, finally, screeching brakes. Somewhere up the tracks, the train shuddered and jerked to an emergency stop.

At the side of the tracks, a stunned-looking couple stood hugging each other. They had abandoned the car just in time. But where was Dwayne?

In the fast-falling snow, Rita couldn't see him, nor could she see the man who had been vainly trying to push the car off the tracks. Then she tripped over something. It was the crumpled body of a man. She bent down and saw the snow covered overcoat. Oh, God! she thought, it's Dwayne! He's dead.

"Dwayne! Dwayne!" she began screaming. The figure on the ground struggled to his knees, almost fell, then tried again and managed to rise to his feet. It was her husband. Hugging him around his neck, Rita burst into tears.

"I'm OK. Calm down, honey. Where's the man who was trying to push the car?"

"I haven't seen him."

Dwayne, the assistant manager from the inn, and several guests organized a search. The sound of the screeching train brakes had brought everyone out of the inn. The trainmen who had run back to the crossing helped them comb each side of the tracks, thinking that the man had been dragged along by the train. The inn sent a thermos of coffee out to the trainmen. They continued searching, but whoever had been trying to push the car off the tracks was nowhere to be found. The train went on.

By now the snow was fluttering lazily down in great flakes, the fierceness of the wind had abated, and visibility was greatly improved. But no body—alive or dead—could be found. Finally, with wet, snow-encrusted shoes and clothing, the Doughtrys and the other guests who had helped search went back in the inn and sat around the fire.

When the assistant manager of the inn joined them, Dwayne was saying, "I thought I could push him off the track and save him. Should we look more?"

"There is no need to," said the assistant manager, his eyes dark and strange.

"But he could be dying out there somewhere," persisted Rita.

"I don't think so," he said. "Do you remember my mentioning on the tour that our former manager, John DuBois, was killed a few years ago in front of the inn?"

"Yes," said Dwayne. "But what does a badly injured man lying out there somewhere in the snow have to do with . . ."

"With John DuBois? Well, there was a late March snowstorm much like this one. John was trying to push a stalled car off the tracks when the train struck him."

"When you left the inn tonight . . . ," the assistant manager seemed reluctant to continue.

"Yes . . . what about it?"

"I think that what you saw was the ghost of John DuBois out there on the tracks."

"His ghost! Good Lord! Now I understand. Part of his face was gone!" Dwayne shuddered.

"Yes, we found him that way."

"Seeing his face was such a shock that I threw myself back from the tracks. That's why the train didn't hit me."

His eyes were filled with awe. The man whose life he had been trying to save was already dead!

John Stone's Inn is located at 179 Main Street in Ashland, Massachusetts. For reservations, call (508) 881–1778.

ABOUT THE AUTHOR

Nancy Roberts is the author of more than twenty books, most pertaining to the supernatural. She has been named "custodian of the twilight zone" by *Southern Living* magazine. A journalist for many years, she has worked for newspapers in New Jersey, Florida, and North Carolina. Her thorough research has won her the Certificate of Commendation from the American Association of State and Local History. Ms. Roberts lives in Charlotte, North Carolina, with her son, David, and her husband, Jim Brown.